# CHRISTMAS

# IN OTHER WORDS

by Maryel Stone

## DEDICATION

To the family of God. In every church, in every denomination, in every home, on every continent, we are all adopted into one family in Him. May this book brighten your Christmas and shine His Light into every dark corner.

# ACKNOWLEDGMENTS

Without Pastor Elliott's encouragement, I would not be a published author today. Although he died before anything with my name on it was in print, he had every confidence that it would happen.

His family, brother, daughters, and nephews are still my family. And always will be.

My sister, Beth, is my spiritual teacher and guardian.

My husband, Rich, and daughter, Alicia, are patient, steadfast, and forgiving.

The family of God cannot be stopped by death or disease. Let us carry on loving and serving God and our neighbors.

# CONTENTS

# INTRODUCTION

When we moved from Pennsylvania to Virginia, we were welcomed to a new church by a new pastor. Pastor Edwin P. Elliott Jr was a fierce Bible scholar, a terrible singer, and a gentle, soft-voiced friend who had no doubts about the love of Jesus. In his tiny church by the railroad tracks, our family became family with his, joined in love and fellowship.

His Christmas Eve tradition was not a formal service, but instead, a simple, child-friendly time of sharing Christmas verses, singing carols, and sitting in the dark, quiet church to listen to a story.

Pastor Elliott's mother wrote some of the stories. Others had been gathered from here and there over the years of the family's ministry from Paris, MO, to Gettysburg, PA, to Water Valley, MS, to Manassas, VA.

When Pastor Elliott found out that I was a would-be writer, he invited me to write a story or two to add to the collection.

So, I did.

The first story I ever shared is the last one in this collection, "My Father's Voice." It is both a Christmas story and my testimony. The story captures the anxious yearning of a young heart for the true peace found only in Jesus Christ. It shares my memories of that moment when I truly heard God's message for the first time.

I hope your church has a similar tradition. I hope you can set aside a time to read these stories out loud to your congregation, or, at home, to your own children. I hope they spark the Spirit of the season within you and bring a smile to your face.

I hope you never forget that the true gift of Christmas arrived in a stable. That baby, raised by ordinary people, welcomed by angels singing, and given gifts from three wise delivery men is our world's Light. I pray that you listen to these words and to the stories and songs of Christmas with your heart.

Maryel Stone

# EVERYDAY MIRACLES

*"I am Gabriel," replied the angel. "I stand in the presence of God, and I was sent to speak to you and to bring you this good news. And now you will be silent and unable to speak until the day this comes to pass, because you did not believe my words, which will be fulfilled at their proper time."*
*Luke 1:19-20*

*I've always been fascinated by the idea of Zechariah, father of John the Baptist, returning from his duties in the Holy of Holies after having been struck mute by the Angel Gabriel. He'd received the best news he could ever have from God's messenger, but it didn't make him happy. It made him angry. Bitter. When we meet him again in scripture, he has completely changed.*

*Here's my idea of what might have been happening in Zechariah's heart.*

My wife is watching me from her chair. She pretends to pick apart the uneven strands from the shawl she's weaving for her cousin, but I've caught her eye more than once. She's been watching me a lot these days. She's worried. Since I lost my words, since they were taken from me, she's been hovering a little closer, making sure to

1

keep her eye on me. I don't mind.

Her eyes are kind, warm and compassionate whenever they look at me. Dark golden, the color of burnt honey. When we first met, formally introduced at our betrothal, not like nowadays, when she was so young and I was so, well, me I remember thinking how they sparkled. Her eyes. One glance and I was smitten. Smitten? Does anyone use that word anymore? Doesn't matter. I like it. It's a good word. The perfect one. 'Struck down by a firm blow.' Yes. Exactly.

Her eyes have always been better than mine.

It's funny. You'd think I'd be the one worried. After all, a man of my age knows that he has far fewer years ahead of him than behind. All the young faces in worship tell me this. Those I'll forever think of as children having children of their own. But, no, I'm not worried. Not about me. I know what comes next, and what a blessing that is.

I lean my head on one hand and look at my wife. Since it happened, since my words became tied up inside my mind, my spirit has been calm. Contented. As if, for the first time in this long, pious life I've lived, I realize that God has me firmly, gently, safely in his grip. And my Elizabeth, too.

It is a unique way to live. To see God moving all around me. You'd think a man like me, raised in my family, in the temple, with tradition and study, praise and prophecy in my blood would have eyes trained to see and ears trained to hear all of the subtle signs of God's presence. That I'd feel his touch on the world all around us. That I'd revel in the evidence of His hand of healing as well as his sword of wrath and proudly point them out to others.

Instead, it's always been Elizabeth. My beautiful bride was the one who would point out the bright red blooms of calanit peeking through fields of grain, or the brilliance of the stars on a particularly cold night, or the abundance of blessings to be found in the humble gift of a pauper's widow. Even with my much-respected education, my pride of place within our community, and my responsibility in the church, it's my wife who truly sees God.

"Everyday miracles," she would say with a smile. "Those are what I look for, husband. Not signs and wonders."

Everyday miracles. Eyes opening to another dawn. Safety when traveling. A warm hearth. Friends. A full belly. Elizabeth's hand in mine at the end of the day. All things I had overlooked. Until now. Until my world was changed by God's messenger. By a promise unfulfilled and a blessing I had given up looking for years ago.

Did you ever hear the saying, "a little learning is a dangerous thing?" That was me. Yes, I knew the sacred scriptures. I could draw the lineage of each priest, each king, and each prophet from Adam to Aphras. The poetry of David and Solomon was often on my lips, and I was trusted with the holy things in the holy places. But even these things, even the knowledge of Jehovah and the wisdom of His message and the business of His ministry can become a veil between one's soul and God's presence. A veil of pride. Of self-importance. As if God's call on my life, the responsibilities, and outright gifts he'd given me had elevated me to His side. Fellow King and Prophet.

The veil between my eyes – my soul – and Jehovah God

wrapped around my head until it glinted like a crown. A crown I'd hammered into shape with harsh words and an arrogant spirit and set upon my own head.

My wife, my Elizabeth, well, her beautiful eyes have always been clear. Unveiled. She'd kept them that way with an open heart, gratitude, and humility of spirit.

Through the best and the worst of times, she finds something to delight in, some small gift dropped from God's hand to be grateful for. Every day. Every hour. When we were first wed, she delighted in every new discovery. After a year, while my status – and my worry – grew, she found more reasons to rejoice. Through her decades of prayer, of waiting, of empty, childless arms, and a silent home, and the careless, hurtful remarks of others, she was grateful to God.

I am ashamed to admit that her contentment often irritated me.

Why wouldn't she rage? Why didn't her anger smolder and burn like mine? Why didn't her heart grow as cold and bitter and unbelieving as my own? A childless home – and me, a priest. Every morning tasted like ashes in my mouth. Every evening, I avoided her gaze across our table. Blamed her. Blamed God.

How could she insist with the same faith, a faith so deep and so wide that it would never drain dry, that God would have His own way and that it would be for our good?

Just a few months ago, it was my turn to serve, to stand within the holiest place and burn the offering. My robes had been brushed, the tassels measured, the ephod shining with the labor of Elizabeth's hands. I had walked past the penitents, my head high, my mind focused on my duty, while my soul grumbled within me with the same old demands and accusations.

"Why, O Lord? Why have you cursed me with a barren wife? Am I not upright? Am I not faithful?"

My unspoken words seemed to rise to heaven with the scent of the incense. And, suddenly, in a beam of golden light and with a rush of wind, I was given an answer.

God's messenger appeared before me, and I shook with fear. Until I die, I will never forget his words:

"Do not be afraid, Zechariah; your prayer has been heard. Your wife Elizabeth will bear you a son, and you are to call him John. He will be a joy and delight to you, and many will rejoice because of his birth, for he will be great in the sight of the Lord. He is never to take wine or other fermented drink, and he will be filled with the Holy Spirit even before he is born. He will bring back many of the people of Israel to the Lord their God. And he will go on before the Lord, in the spirit and power of Elijah, to turn the hearts of the parents to their children and the disobedient to the wisdom of the righteous; to make ready a people prepared for the Lord."

A messenger from God. Words spoken from Heaven. Oh, how richly I had been blessed. My spirit soared. My heart swelled with joy.

I sigh to myself. If only. If only that had been my response to the Lord my God's messenger. If only I could go back to that moment and take back the foolish, arrogant words that sprang from my mouth.

I will never forget, nor forgive myself, for my answer:

"How can I be sure of this?" I confronted Jehovah's messenger. "I am an old man, and my wife is well along in years."

All my life I had looked for signs and wonders, never content with my wife's "everyday miracles." And yet, here stood Gabriel, an angel of the Lord, bringing me the news that I had coveted for decades. And still I doubted. Still, I lifted my chin and demanded more of God.

And He, Jehovah God, condescended to give me yet another gift:

"And now you will be silent and not able to speak until the day this happens, because you did not believe my words, which will come true at their appointed time," Gabriel replied. And then he was gone.

Now, it's my turn to watch. To let all my fears and doubts dissolve, unspoken, while I watch the miracles that God gives. Now I watch my lovely wife. I look on her steady hands at her work, the peace and joy that surround her, the faint smile that lingers on her lips. Our child, promised by the Lord God Himself, grows healthy and strong in her belly. And now my unbelieving lips are sealed by that same God, my resentful laughter and frigid disbelief silenced, and I find I am more content and hopeful than I have ever been.

I'm grateful that my wife couldn't hear my mocking words within Jehovah's holy place. That my shame was revealed to Jehovah God alone. Even at my worst, God gave me, gave us, another everyday miracle when his messenger sent me out to greet my wife with tears of awe and joy rather than an arrogant speech filled with distrust. He didn't let me hurt my Elizabeth with my doubt.

I'd gladly remain mute for the rest of my life rather than utter one syllable that doubts my faithful God or hurts my loving wife.

And when my child is born, as he will be soon, and he takes my hand and looks to me to teach him about our God, I will gladly use every sense God provides to tell him of joy, of faithfulness, of glory, majesty, and truth. Of his promised role to turn the hearts of Israel back to their Creator and King. Of the coming Messiah. I'll treasure each everyday miracle of my son's life. And I'll pray that I'm found faithful enough to raise this new Elijah. My son. John.

Elizabeth has caught me watching her, now, and she's smiling at me. I rise to go to her, to take her hand and help her from her chair. Her cousin, Mary, is arriving soon. There is some great news that she wishes to tell us. I wonder, as I lead my wife to our night's rest, if this will be another everyday miracle that God grants us. Or, perhaps, something more.

Whichever it is, I'll praise God for it. For love. For faith. For family. For children's voices and a foolish old man's silence. For the fulfillment of every single promise God has made. For flowers and stars, honey-colored eyes, and the warmth of my Elizabeth's hand in mine. For a quiet and contrite heart and the wonder of birth.

# MY LITTLE LIGHT

*We've been taught since childhood to let our little lights shine. Some of us remember the song, and some of us are still lighting those flames, one simple act of kindness at a time.*

The icy rain had stopped, giving Angie's worn wipers a break. They'd been squeaking and groaning for miles as they strained to compete with the freezing rain. She wiggled her cramped fingers, trying to loosen her death-grip on the steering wheel. Holding it tighter wasn't going to help her get home.

She should have left earlier. Ducked out of work after lunch like so many of the others did with a wink and a finger to their lips. Angie couldn't afford to lose the hours – or the job if the boss dropped in to count heads.

"It's Christmas Eve. Old Denise Scrooge should give us the afternoon." She'd heard it over and over again. Around the coffee pot. In the rest room. Along the corridors outside the sales office. "It's not like anyone's in here shopping for a car. Not today."

Angie had smiled and kept her head down. In her experience, 'shoulds' rarely became reality.

Her husband should have hung around after Jimmy was born. He should have kept off drugs, kept a job, and paid his child support. Angie's previous boss should have understood when Jimmy got sick, and she had to miss so much work. The holiday traffic out of the city should have already tapered off when she finally pulled away from home at 7:30 pm.

"Oh, no, Angie," she chided herself. "This will not become a poor-me moment." She chuckled. "Too movie-of-the-week for words."

Thankful. That's what she intended to be. Angie straightened her shoulders. This Christmas she would exude gratitude. Beam it out through her pores, gosh darn it. Not one word of complaint would pass these lips.

Angie sighed and turned the music down another click. Internal rant over, she decided. If she couldn't be grateful on Christmas Eve, when could she be grateful?

"Mommy?"

She glanced in the rearview mirror, smiling at the sight of Jimmy's big brown eyes shining back at her.

"Hey, I thought you were asleep."

"Not sleepy, Mommy." He kicked his legs. "Are we there soon?"

"Pretty soon, buddy. Ten more minutes."

He laughed. It was their little joke. Whenever Jimmy asked how long it would take to get where they were going, or when dinner would be ready, or if it were time to watch his favorite show, or when Angie would hang up from work calls, the standard answer was ten more minutes.

This time, it wasn't far off. Hopefully. She flicked her signal and turned off the main road into her parents' neighborhood. Squinting through the dim light of her slush-coated headlights and the atmospheric street lamps, her stomach churned.

Away from the main highway, the valley where her parents lived was filled with fog. Like a lake of white smoke, it ate her headlights as she inched down the hill. She flipped on her high beams and quickly switched them off again, trying to blink away the reflection that the fog threw back at her.

It really was only about ten minutes to her parents' house. If she could see the way.

She crept along, focusing on the white line at the edge of the road. It was an old trick her father had taught her, helping her navigate in harsh conditions.

There would be a haven up ahead. A reminder of her own childhood. One more cross-street.

Angie groaned. At the corner, the local market's sign was dark.

"Mommy?"

She paused a little longer at the stop sign. "Sorry, buddy. Looks like we'll have to try on the way home in a couple of days." She'd promised him a trip to the tiny market, telling him about the penny candy she used to buy, the long red licorice whips and the Mary Janes, how she and her friends would hike all the way up the hill to the store and come back with warm bottles of cream soda and sticky fingers. It had seemed like such an adventure.

"Okay, Mommy." Jimmy grinned.

Wow. Angie's heart swelled, just like in a movie. "You're a great kid, you know that?"

Pulling away, Angie lightened up on the gas as the back tire spun on an icy patch. She breathed a quick prayer of thanks when the nearly bald surface found purchase again. The main roads had been wet but safe. Or as safe as they could be when they carried hundreds of cars filled with impatient, tired, over-caffeinated drivers anxious to get home. These side roads, though. She slowed further. She couldn't trust them.

Especially when she couldn't see more than two feet in front of her.

"Mommy? Can we sing?"

Angie turned the music up again, recognizing the familiar tune as one of Jimmy's favorites. "Sure, we can."

The words were simple, easy for a three-year-old. The song one she remembered from her own childhood. She and her sisters had sung about their little lights shining, holding up one finger as a candle and puffing on it to mock blowing it out.

Jimmy's sweet voice filled the car, bringing a huge grin to her face. "Again, again!"

Angie laughed, clicking the button. "Sure, buddy. One more time."

When they'd finished the chorus, Angie switched to another

playlist. "How about some Christmas songs?"

When she looked up, the fog in front of her swirled, a blacker patch of night dead ahead.

Controlled, she eased down on the brakes. She knew better than to stomp on them.

The rear-end fishtailed a bit but settled down quick.

Brilliant green eyes shined through the fog, staring at her, before blinking out, the dark bulk of the deer walking calmly across the road in the wash of her headlights.

"A deer!"

"That's right," Angie agreed, her voice a little hoarse with shock. "Did you see its tail?"

"Flip-flip goes the tail," Jimmy recited. He leaned sideways trying to reach his favorite book on the seat next to him, but the car seat wouldn't budge. "Mommy?"

"Almost there, sweetie. Come on, one more song."

She eased the car ahead, heart still pounding against her chest. She sang along, the words of the old carol as familiar to her as her name. It was easy to send up a prayer while she kept the song going. A prayer she'd prayed many times. That had never been unanswered.

"Dear Lord, help me find my way home."

Her answer shined through the fog, white and warm and comforting.

Turning onto her parents' street, Angie blinked tears from her eyes.

Lined up and down the street, paper bags glowed like promises in the dark.

Luminarias. Simple bags filled with sand, holding a single candle. They lit up a pathway for her to follow.

"Mommy! Little lights!"

"Yeah," Angie breathed, laughing. "Little lights."

With Jimmy singing behind her, Angie let the car drift down the street. The Porters' bags were decorated with stars. The Wilsons' with mangers. Nancy and Sam's were plain. At every house, along the edge of every yard, the luminaria's glowed.

They must have waited until the rain stopped. She imagined every neighbor, every family leaving their warm homes, putting on boots and gloves, and struggling through the dark to light their candles.

Outside Widow Nicholson's house, a figure in a dark parka was bent over the last lightless luminaria, flicking a long grill lighter.

Jimmy shrieked, clapping as the candle caught and the figure straightened, waving.

"Hi! Hi!" Jimmy called.

Angie peered through the dark, recognizing her father's face.

Her father had done this. Organized the neighborhood. Asked them to light Angie's way home. Or, maybe, her father had trudged up and down the street lighting each one himself.

She laughed. "Look, Jimmy! It's grandpa!"

"Grampa!" Jimmy kicked his legs.

Her father grinned and shook his head, gesturing Angie down the street.

At the top of the last little hill, she had to stop. Not because the fog thickened. Not because her tires slid, or another deer crossed the street. Angie stopped to raise her aching hands from the steering wheel and give thanks. Because she'd prayed and her Father had sent her a safe way home.

There, before them, all the little lights of her family and neighbors shined. Leading them. Making sure she could find her way.

"Mommy?"

"Let your light shine," Angie said.

Before Jimmy sang one verse, they were home. Safe. The front curtains were open, and her family's tree twinkled, the star on top blazing.

"It's Christmas, Mommy! The star!"

Angie hauled Jimmy up from his car seat and turned so he could see the tree, the star, and the lights of the neighborhood glowing through the fog.

"It sure is, buddy. The star, the light, showed us the way."

# THE DELIVERY MEN, REDUX

*Long before I joined the tiny church by the railroad tracks, the story of two delivery men hauling a new television and a coffee table around on Christmas Eve was a congregation favorite. Unfortunately, over the years, the last page of the story was lost, and the ending of a different story inserted. Strangely, our congregation didn't seem to notice, in fact, the garbled story has been read many times and the ending shrugged off as 'unique' or 'charming.'*

*I decided to try my hand at a modern re-telling of that beloved tale. I hope I did it justice.*


"Any luck?"

Ganz didn't look up from organizing the packages in the back of his truck. The loaders had their system, but he had his. And his was better. "I haven't come across it, no."

"Look, I know you're busy."

Ganz laid the handheld on top of a box and turned. "I am busy. We're all busy, Mel." He waved his arms at the bustling loading dock of the shipping warehouse. "It's Christmas Eve and it's snowing and we'd all like to get finished at a reasonable hour. So, if you could stop making Mrs. Josephs and her lost package my problem, that would be great." He snorted. "You've heard the expression, right?"

Mel grinned, setting his cap higher on his head. "How could I not? You say it all the time, Ganz!"

From around the loading dock, six other drivers chimed up in unison. "'Not my circus, not my monkeys!'"

Ganz shook his head, chuckling along with them. "I guess I do say it a lot." He pointed. "But that doesn't make it less true."

"I don't know." Mel shoved his hands into his pockets, shoulders up around his ears. "I kind of feel that this is our circus, Ganz. I mean, these packages, seeing that our customers get what they order on time. It is up to us."

Miriam jogged past, arms waving up and down, scratching her side, making monkey noises.

"You definitely are not my monkey!" Ganz shouted. "Someone get the ringmaster. Or the animal trainer. One's got loose."

"Ooo -ooo -ooo." Monkey calls echoed from all around.

"No extras on my truck, Mel." Miriam called back over her shoulder.

"Thanks for checking, Mir!" the driver shouted back.

As others checked in with Mel, Ganz turned back to his organizing. "Three, two, one. Good. That's that then." He hooked the bungee cords across the packages, now lined up so that he could easily see which was next on his route. He grabbed the strap and rolled the door down, stepping back out of the truck and onto the dock.

Mel was frowning over his clipboard.

"Have you checked with Hazard?"

Setting his finger on the page to keep his place, Mel raised his eyes, and his eyebrows.

"You think that's a good idea?"

Ganz peered into the warehouse. He sighted his target high on a warehouse rolling ladder, headphones mashing down his curly hair, so it stuck out in all directions. "Everybody says Hazard has the worst record of losing packages. What they don't mention is that the guy takes on everyone's worst lost package problems, so his stats are all out of whack. And, you know what? He finds more than anyone else, too."

"I never thought of that." Mel cocked his head. "I should head out, but …"

Slapping his friend on the back, Ganz said, "Hazard isn't good with the face-to-face stuff. That's why he wears headphones. Just text him the details. Tell him about Mrs. Josephs' little boy. How the dad has been deployed and won't get back for Christmas. That package was logged in here, when?"

"A week ago," Mel groaned.

Ganz winced. The longer a package went missing, the more likely it was never going to be found. It had probably made its way into an employee's pocket. Or had been shoved onto the returns shelf and sent back. "Hazard is your best bet."

"Thanks." Mel shook Ganz's hand before hurrying back to his

own truck.

Climbing behind the wheel, Ganz set his handheld in its dock and started the engine. He set the heat to low – why bother heating up the cab when every time he opened the door the windows would fog up. He wriggled his toes in his thermal socks and rubbed his thick gloved hands together. "Warm feet, warm hands, all set."

Midmorning, the snow was still coming down. Luckily, the ground was warm, too warm to let the roads get slick. Still, Ganz was careful, keeping his speed sensible. He had a half-full truck still to deliver and he was not going to be the guy that ruined some kid's Christmas by smashing his truck into a tree.

His thoughts circled back to Mel's anxious face on the loading dock. Sure, Ganz liked his systems, his rituals, but he had a soft side, too. Mel, on the other hand had a warm squishy center, like Ganz's wife's favorite Mallomars. Maybe it was because Mel rarely got to see his daughter on Christmas, now that the divorce was final, and his wife moved out of state. Mel couldn't look at a single parent at this time of year without feeling for them.

Especially someone like Mary Josephs. Young when she married her soldier sweetheart, she'd had her son just about nine months after he'd shipped out for a two year tour. Her folks were out west somewhere, not exactly delighted by their daughter's decisions. They didn't like the military, didn't agree with Mary putting off college. They thought their daughter could do better than raising a jarhead's son outside the base in Virginia.

The Josephs' house was on the eastern route that Ganz and Mel worked. With a young one, Mary did a lot of her shopping on-line. Everything from diapers to groceries to the kid's clothes came in cardboard boxes and pouches delivered to her doorstep. Both drivers liked getting to know their regular customers. Not to mention that Mary's home baked goodies she left out for them made her a definite stand-out.

Hurrying back to the truck after another delivery, Ganz's phone beeped. Mel was texting.

"Hazard on it. Says he's got a lead. Said to check back after lunch."

Ganz tugged his glove off with his teeth and texted back. "OK. Let me know."

"Tell Mary?"

Ganz hesitated. "Don't get hopes up," he typed.

"OK."

Ganz couldn't take his own advice. The Josephs' house was just two streets over. It wasn't much of a detour. He drove past slowly and caught the moment Mary saw him out the front window. He slowed, shaking his head. Dang it. He should have kept going.

Mary had the front door open by the time he stopped. She nearly slipped on an icy patch on her sidewalk before she steadied herself.

Ganz opened the truck's door, ready to leap out to help. "You okay?"

"Fine, yes! Did Mel find it?"

Her cheeks were pink as she shivered in her shirtsleeves and jeans. "Not yet, but we've got the best lost package finder in the warehouse on it. Just wanted you to know we haven't forgotten."

"Oh, I knew that. You are both so kind to help me." Her dark hair drifted around her face as she shook her head. "And Christmas Eve. You should both be more worried about getting back to your families instead of my silly package."

"We'll make it home in time, don't you worry. Mel will let you know when we've got it." He started to close the door again.

"Wait!"

Mary grabbed something off her porch and slid down the sidewalk towards him.

"Here. And please give this one to Mel just in case I don't see him later."

Two packages, wrapped in brown paper and tied with string. "That's very kind, ma'am. I sure will."

He didn't want to encourage her to stay outside any longer, so Ganz closed the door and slid the truck into gear, waving back at her smiling face.

It was customers like Mary Josephs that made this job worth the hours, the stress, and the not-so-nice interactions.

Ganz tried to put the young mom out of his thoughts and got on with his other deliveries.

By three-thirty, the light snow had turned into sleet and the sky was as dark as midnight. Ganz pulled up to his last stop, maneuvering the truck so that the side door opened at the end of the sidewalk. He shut off the motor.

At least twenty-four by twenty-four, the box looked like it would weigh a ton, but Ganz knew from shoving it around in the back that it was light, as if filled with air. He tugged it closer to the edge and bent his knees. No reason to take chances with his back on the last package.

"Need any help?"

Ganz peered around the edge of the box. "I've got it, Reverend. It's not heavy at all."

"Oh, I'm so relieved." Reverend Post sighed. "The kids would have been disappointed."

"Yeah?" Ganz followed the minister up the sidewalk and waited for him to open the door. "I've been trying to figure out what it could be." He chuckled. "I'm guessing you wouldn't be so happy to see a box of toilet paper or paper cups."

Post cocked his head. "At times I have rejoiced over both those deliveries."

"Where do you want this?" Ganz offered.

"Right here is fine. You don't have to –"

Reverend Post looked to weigh in at about ninety-eight pounds. There was no way Ganz was going to let him try to wrangle this thing down the long hall to his office. He glanced down. Oh. Maybe he shouldn't walk down there either; his shoes were trailing slush all over the carpeting.

"Look, how about we just open it here?" Ganz set the box on the edge of a low table.

"Good idea." Post snatched up the can that was covered with a childish drawing and the note, 'Pennies for the Poor,' and moved it out of the way.

Ganz fished his box cutter from his belt and slit the tape. Opening the flaps, he dragged out a sleeve of packing bubbles. And then another one. "Huh. I wasn't far off thinking you ordered some air." Finally, he reached the well-wrapped item inside.

Reverend Post accepted it with a smile. "Yes. The perfect one."

At least eighteen inches from point to point, the star was made of cloudy plastic, a long white cord dangling from the bottom.

"Our Christmas star burned out night before last. I was worried we wouldn't have a replacement in time for Christmas Eve service tonight."

"It's, ah, nice," Ganz muttered.

Laughing, Post scratched at the wavy surface. "No, it isn't. But it exactly matches the one that's stood over our manger since my father was pastor here. Especially at this time of year, people need nostalgia. They need to feel that things haven't changed. Even when they have." He paused. "Especially when they have."

"I get that."

"Where are you spending Christmas Eve?" the reverend asked. "You and your family are welcome here."

"Um, thanks." Ganz nodded towards the open door to the sanctuary. "Haven't been to church in a long while. I think I've forgotten how."

"How to what?" Post asked. "How to sit? How to sing Christmas carols? Listen to stories? To pray?"

Ganz rubbed the back of his neck. "Um –"

Post cradled the cheap-looking star to his chest and held out his hand. "I didn't mean to make you uncomfortable. Merry Christmas. And thank you for this."

"Pastor – maybe you could say a little prayer for me?"

"Of course."

Post waited expectantly, their hands still clasped, his eyes kind while Ganz hesitated.

"One of my customers. She's on her own with a little boy. The package from her husband, he's deployed, it's gone missing. She was really looking forward to it."

The reverend nodded and then bowed his head.

Ganz tried to step back but the pastor's grip held him. He hadn't meant the man would pray now.

"Dear Father, He who has given us the greatest gift of all in his precious Son, please bless this man and his family. And bless this young mother and her son, alone on Christmas Eve. Send your angels with this package, this message of love as you did all those years ago in Bethlehem. Grant them great gifts, dear Lord, of peace and love and hope in you. Better than any gold, frankincense, and myrrh. Amen."

Mumbling his thanks, Ganz hurried back to his truck. He fishtailed pulling out too fast before he steadied himself and took a deep breath. "Okay. Back to the warehouse and then home." And maybe, he thought, maybe he'd take the kids to church. Check out what that old star looked like all lit up.

It couldn't hurt.

Before Ganz could shut off the truck, Mel hurled himself at his door, waving a flat brown-paper-wrapped package.

"You found it!"

"Hazard did! That guy is a miracle worker!"

Ganz felt a warmth in his chest. "Miracle. Yeah, just about." The truck lurched into park, and he grabbed Mel before he could fall. "Well? Aren't you going over to the Josephs?"

"Fool's truck won't start." Hazard had dropped his headphones around his neck and was bundled up in a quilted blue puffer coat. "And he was going to give me a ride home."

There was only one thing Ganz could do.

Twenty minutes later, he pulled his SUV into Mary Josephs' driveway. All the lights were on, the Christmas tree blinking in the front window every color of the rainbow. Mary held Junior in her arms, the little boy reaching towards the shiny ornaments. She glanced out the window, frowning, until she recognized Ganz and Mel – and Hazard - in their distinctive uniforms. Her mouth dropped open.

She met them at the door.

A few minutes later, the three loaded back in Ganz's car, Hazard still silently in awe of the huge plate of cookies in his lap.

"Nice lady," he finally mumbled around a full mouth.

"Yeah. Imagine being so excited about something like that."

"And so worried it wouldn't get there on time."

Ganz reversed carefully out of the driveway before looking back at Mary's house. Mary was still holding her son, opening and closing the bulky card that had been the only thing in the package.

The package hadn't held the latest gadget or book or bright, shiny toy. It was one of those cards where you could record your voice. Junior's father had recorded a special Christmas message for his son. Mary hadn't wanted him to miss it.

As they pulled away, Ganz cleared his throat. "You guys want to come to church with us tonight?"

Two silent, shocked stares met his.

"Never mind," Ganz sighed.

"Sure."

"What time?"

Huh. Ganz steered towards Hazard's apartment. "I'll pick you guys up at seven. Okay?"

It turned out, that cheap, plastic Christmas star looked pretty good shining over Reverend Post's manger. And Ganz hadn't forgotten how to pray after all.

# ORDINARY PEOPLE

*Did Mary know? Songs have asked that over the centuries since Christ's birth. Of course, she knew. The angel's message was clear, and the words of Mary's Magnificat tell us she wondered and marveled at the miracle. But the echoing words of Scripture and Mary's inspiring reaction couldn't be the whole story. Just as Joseph had doubts, I believe Mary must have had some, too. Not doubts about God's message, but about her own ability to raise the Son of God. A young, inexperienced woman, suddenly pregnant with her own redeemer. Imagine.*

He's sleeping, now. My baby. My son. Red-faced from crying, his breaths come in little hops and skips, tiny fists curled against his cheeks. So small. So fragile. So perfect. I'm afraid to move, to make a sound, afraid he'll wake up again and those eyes will pierce me through, demanding that I make his world right. Me. A brand new mother alone out here in the barn with a brand-new father beside me. Neither of us with much of an idea what to do, or how to do this. How to be what he needs.

I'm afraid to move, but I do. Shifting slowly to sit beside the manger, I trace one finger across his forehead and down his cheek, barely touching him. He's beautiful. But maybe I'm biased. Maybe all new mothers feel this way. Elizabeth did. I remember her childbed, the way Zechariah had knelt at her side, silently praying, his eyes wide with wonder as the tiny screaming infant was placed in his arms. I thought the child ugly and wrinkled, like a shriveled date, but Elizabeth had pronounced him perfect and handsome, and her husband had shouted with joy.

Yesterday, exhausted and limp in my own childbed, my eyes filled with tears when Joseph placed my son on my chest. Joseph's hands were bloody as they wrapped the boy in the clean cloths the innkeeper's wife gave us. The baby had been squalling and messy, tiny arms and legs jerking, his face screwed up with cold and fear. Wrinkled, his head shaped like a cone, my babe had been no more sweet or handsome than Elizabeth's John. But, after I had put him to my breast, after the first panic and excitement passed – for mother and child – he changed. Changed from a strange, shrieking thing to this soft, precious child. My child. My son. Nothing could be more beautiful.

The journey was hard. We had so far to go. Relaxing now against the pile of hay Joseph had gathered into a bed, I have trouble remembering much of it. That is a blessing, I think. I don't want to remember mile after mile of hard road beneath the donkey's hoofs, each step sending a sharp jolt along my spine. I don't need to remember how pale Joseph's face became beneath the dust, how he leaned more heavily on his staff at the end of each day. His sandal strap had broken two days ago, and the sole is now tied around his foot with rope. And yet he still works to make sure this rough barn is warm enough for his new son.

I tugged the rough blanket higher, shivering a little. Joseph is busy with a pot of water over the firepot, a heavy metal vessel that a shepherd had brought, the coals within it warm and red. The innkeeper had frowned at first, afraid for his barn, for his animals and livelihood, but his wife had taken him aside and whispered sharply in his ear and he'd been content to lecture Joseph about the fire and its care.

I can feel the smile on my face as I watch my husband, this new father. No one is more careful than Joseph. All this time, through all the strange and wondrous changes that have come upon us both, he has made sure to care for me, and now, for this child.

Our child.

Somehow, some way, our child.

The shepherds came last night, in twos and threes, their flocks swarming nearby hills. Simple men whose faces were filled with awe, shining with the light of heaven, coming to greet their promised Savior, their King. My son. They said very little but brought what they could. The thick fleece that lies across the baby's chest. Half a bushel of grain. A flask of watered wine. Most of all, they brought their prayers, their praises.

I could only watch silently as God's favor touched each one through a single look at my sleeping babe.

As if drawn by a tight cord, I turned again to the baby. In the quiet while the child sleeps, as I watch his small chest rise and fall, the promises of God's messenger come to my mind. A child. A King. A Savior. The Son of God. Such a weight of glory for such a tiny babe. A weight of glory and the burden of a Kingdom beyond imagining.

The messenger's words became a solace to me on the journey. They soothed my heart during the long nights and my bones during the days of travel. I had little to do but think and remember, to imagine the shining king, the savior of God's promise. I'd wondered if he would look different, if he would be born with knowledge behind his eyes, eyes that could see through to my soul, could see all my doubts, fears, and wonderings. If he would judge my fumbling hands and Joseph's worries. If he would be bigger, stronger than other babes. More beautiful. More serene and wise. If the stamp of God's favor would shine out like golden light.

Once I held him that first time, all I could do was what every mother did. Through tears of relief and a deep, blossoming well of joy I counted.

Two eyes. Dark and warm like my father's. Two ears, tiny shells perfectly formed. A nose, barely there, a bump between two round cheeks. Two arms, two hands, grasping for me. For me, a mother now. His mother, or at least trying my best to be. Two legs and feet, kicking and squirming against me. Ten fingers and ten little toes.

I counted, and so forgot, for a moment, that this baby was different. That he had come to me by God's miraculous hand. That I was not an ordinary mother nor Joseph an ordinary father. For a moment I forgot that this baby was not mine, not ours, not the way an ordinary child belonged to his mother and father, blood, bone, and skin. He was a miracle. A gift.

A gift to the entire world. A gift God placed in my two hands, my ordinary, awkward hands. How could the God of the universe trust me with so precious, so extraordinary a gift?

"Mary?" Joseph knelt beside me, brushing a hand across my wet cheek. "Are you well?"

I turned to kiss his palm, tasting salt. "The Son of God, Joseph. He is the Son of God."

"He is our son, Mary."

"Is he? Is he ours?" I asked, my voice trembling.

He took my hands between his. "He is. He is ours. Our child. Our charge. To love and raise and teach and cherish, for as long as we are given him. Just like any ordinary family."

I shook my head. "Not like any other."

"Maybe not, but God gave this child to you and me, Joseph and Mary, two very ordinary people." His laugh is low and deep. "We can only do what ordinary people do, can't we?"

My stomach churned with fear. "Why did God choose us? He's special and we are not. What can we give this child of God, this Savior? This King?"

Joseph touched my cheek, urging me to turn and look again. The babe had found his fist and was sucking on it, making slurping sounds. "This baby," he reminded me. "This infant."

"For now," I began.

"Now is all that we have. All anyone has." Joseph leaned closer.

"We give him what every father and mother give their children. Because each babe is a gift from God. Each one has a special purpose and plan. You." He smiled and pressed my fingers to his lips. "Me. Our parents. Your cousins." He rolled his eyes. "My unruly nephews. The shepherds who came. Others already on their way. All children are a miracle, Mary."

I know it to be true, but the angel's words echo in my memory.

"He will be great and will be called the Son of the Most High. And the Lord God will give to him the throne of his father David, and he will reign over the house of Jacob forever, and of his kingdom there will be no end."

The Son of God. "Not like him," I replied.

"No." Joseph grunted and sat beside me. He slid one arm around my shoulders, taking a moment of rest for the first time in weeks. "I know of no other baby visited by shepherds kneeling before him. Or greeted by the Gloria of the stars themselves." His eyes shone in wonder. "He has been given amazing gifts and promised amazing things. But our God knows what he is doing. He has given charge of this extraordinary child to ordinary people. Perhaps he wants us to give him the ordinary things of life." Joseph held me close. "Perhaps we are the perfectly ordinary people to do just that."

I remembered faith, and trust, and God's promises – not just for this child, but for me and for Joseph, for shepherds and innkeepers, for wise men and simple, ordinary people. For all the ordinary mothers and fathers who are afraid of making a mistake with their own precious gifts.

"We'll be ordinary together," Joseph promised. "A mother and father seeking to do their best in God's eyes for their child. Trusting in Yahweh to show them the way."

I let the weight of my fears fall away as Joseph's words sank into my spirit. "I can be ordinary," I murmured. "An ordinary mother for an extraordinary child."

# THE KIDS' TABLE

*On October 11, 2009, our beloved pastor died. Writing that date, seeing that it happened 13 years ago, is confounding. To most of us, it feels like it happened both yesterday and a hundred years ago. He was larger than his small stature, a huge presence not only in our church but around the country and the world. Oh, how his light shone.*

*He was only 62. Younger than I am now.*

*That year, his family could not stand to hear a familiar Christmas story. To listen as another voice read beloved words about home, faith, and family. In grieving agreement, I was determined to write a story unlike any other. Without the weight of history, or depth of love and hurt that was predestined to fill our hearts that first Christmas without him.*

*And so, The Kids' Table was born.*

"Let no one despise you for your youth, but set the believers an example in speech, in conduct, in love, in faith, in purity." 1 Timothy 4:12

Jason paused on the next to the last step and closed his eyes. Pine tree scent, check. Christmas carol playlist ringing out, check. The sounds of voices and laughter - kids, parents, spinster aunts and mostly deaf Uncle George hollering over everyone else – check, check, check. He could hear it coming at him from every room. This was the Franklin house at Christmas time, where nothing ever changed. Nothing. Ever.

He hopped down the last few steps and turned left into the living room. Change was too much to expect, he supposed. Jason peered into the sea of festive sweaters and tweed blazers hanging around the punch bowl under the watchful eye of the G. E. angel that had been leaning crookedly from atop the Christmas tree every year for as long as he could remember. He'd just finished his first semester at college. He'd been away from home for four months, taking care of himself, handling classes and a job and normal life pretty well, he thought. A lot had changed for him. But after five minutes back home he'd been reminded that here, among his family, no matter how much time had passed or how many birthdays he counted, as the only child of his parents, he'd always be a kid.

Jason made it through the edges of the crowd with a few smiles and mumbled hellos. Grandma Eleanor gave him a hug and a peppermint. The New York cousins, skinny jeans and plaid shirts and thick-framed glasses worn like some kind of uniform, surrounded him to talk craft beer and Instagram accounts. Jason nodded, hands in his pockets, and slid as smoothly – and slowly – as a glacier into the dining room. There he found it. Parked just east of the family's massive dining room table. The proof that his semi-independence and lofty stature of adulthood had disappeared.

The kids' table.

Six mis-matched chairs around a plastic folding table. Vinyl reindeer-decorated placemats at every place, red paper napkins, and assorted plastic cups were festive enough, but had nothing on the crystal, and china, and cloth napkins in glittering napkin rings on the main table. Jason stared down at the further evidence of his mom's craftiness. He poked a finger into the hollow eye of the cardboard snowman that smiled around his pipe-cleaner pipe and clutched the dreaded place card labeled 'Jason' in its wooly-mittened hands. He felt his lips twist in a wry grin.

"Hey, Google, play Blue Christmas!"

The song changed and suddenly Elvis had been invited to Christmas dinner, too. Jason wouldn't be surprised. This year the Franklin House seemed like the place to be. Every family member, from 92-year-old Great Aunt Sarah to the Atlanta contingent wearing all Bulldog red and Arch black and chortling about the Rose Bowl had accepted his parents' invitation to a 'traditional family Christmas.'

"I know." His father laid a hand on Jason's shoulder from behind, examining the childish place settings. "But someone's got to bite the bullet, son."

Jason shook his head as dad walked on, swiveling his hips along with Elvis. His father had been quick to remind him this morning that the elegant dining room table was a finite space and if they tried to sit one more person there, with the adults, the very universe itself could implode because of Pauli's exclusionary principle or Einstein's theory, or, as Jason wasn't exactly listening in the first place, maybe

Mr. Spock's senior thesis on wormhole physics. Jason shivered. Far be it from him to contradict Mr. Spock.

The snowman smirked up at him with its one remaining eye and Jason sighed. Yep. It was the kids' table for him – again. Just because he thought living away from home might nudge him over the threshold into adulthood didn't guarantee that any other member of the Franklin clan would acknowledge it. Oh, well, he dropped his shoulders into a melodramatic slouch; maybe it wouldn't be that bad this year.

"Hey, Jase."

Then again, maybe it would. Jason turned from his torture of the now winking snowman place card to confront the owner of the sticky voice behind him.

"Frankie," Jason drawled.

There he stood in all his glory – Franklin D. Franklin. An eleven-year-old collection of every murky strand of DNA and personality defect that had ever surfaced in the Franklin family gene pool. Jason laid most of the blame at the feet of Frankie's parents – Aunt Virginia and Uncle Jack – who had saddled their son with the most redundant name since Galileo Galilei. Galileo, Jason surmised, had never had to contend with school bus bullies or the occasional sight of his own jockey shorts flapping from the top of the flagpole. But Frankie's parents had also insisted on dressing their son like a rhinestone cowboy, complete with steel-tipped boots, fringed jackets, and an unfortunately diverse collection of bolo ties. They had, thereby, consigned their only child to one of two schoolyard classifications: perpetual victim or bad-tempered bully.

"Yikes, with that hair I thought you were a girl for a minute there," Frankie chuckled, the fat fingers of one hand wrapped around an oversized candy cane.

No great surprise which stereotype little Frankie fell into. Seven years younger and still the kid could dredge up fond, nostalgic memories of steamy locker rooms filled with sweaty jocks, wedgies, and massive feelings of inferiority. Was Galileo a bully, Jason wondered, before idly considering whether or not a steady diet of country music led to brain damage.

"You're short," Jason replied obliquely, shoving both hands back into the pockets of his jeans to remove the temptation of wrapping his fingers around his cousin's throat. The kid's neck had to be in there somewhere between the cow skull bolo tie and the proudly jutting chin.

The candy cane endured some more abuse as if Frankie could suck some wit out of the red and white sweet, and Jason watched his cousin's eyes narrow in concentration. Jason stood patiently, rocking slightly up and down on his toes, waiting. Waiting. Waiting... C'mon, kid, don't strain something, he thought. The candy cane was finally pulled from Frankie's sticky mouth with a loud pop.

"My momma says if a guy's hair is longer than his collar, he's a momma's boy."

Jason could only blink a moment at the irony. He let his gaze linger on the kid's blond buzz cut before trailing it down the blue and black plaid shirt straining at its mother-of-pearl buttons, pausing at the oversized belt-buckle in the shape of stampeding horses, down the starched jeans to the steel tips of the carved cowboy boots. "I suggest she take the matter up with Troy Polamalu and then get back to me."

He strode towards the punch bowl figuring he could grab a handful of Chex mix, a cup of eggnog, and probably re-read War and Peace before Frankie's lightning-fast intellect caught up with that one.

"Robert – where did you get these glasses? Ellie - Eleanor!" Grandpa Eddie grabbed at the sleeve of his wife's red, reindeer infested sweater and waved his cup of eggnog through the air. "Ellie– look at these glasses – look!"

Grandma Eleanor took a step backwards to avoid the wave of thick yellow liquid that punctuated Eddie's outburst and sloshed onto the pale grey carpeting at her feet.

"Oops, sorry," Jason's grandfather laughed, clutching one antler of the moose head glass he was still brandishing towards his wife.

Jason made a swift detour to the kitchen to pick up a wet towel and gave his mother a quick hug from behind to thank her for being so normal... considering.

"Jason!" The shriek was ear-splitting. "You made me lose count!" His mother huffed loudly and plucked the cucumber slices from the top of the large salad bowl and began again. "One, two, three…"

Mostly normal, anyway, Jason thought. Ducking warily under Grandpa Eddie's waving arms, Jason bent to wipe up the stain while trying to tune out references to the 'jelly of the month club' and whether or not squirrels really are high in cholesterol, hoping that someone would get the man off of his favorite Christmas movie before Jason was wearing his next glass of eggnog in his apparently too long hair.

"Oh, what a nice boy you've raised, Robert," Great Aunt Sarah gushed as Jason climbed to his feet. "Didn't even have to be told, did you, sweetie?"

Jason smiled down... and down... at the tiny old woman, leaning over as the wrinkled hand rose to pat him on the cheek. At least she didn't –

"Ow!"

- pinch, he thought grimly, rubbing one hand along the offended area as he turned to keep an eye on Aunt Sissy who stood smirking at his back. And wasn't THAT name the worst pairing of personality and title in the history of names everywhere? With her wide shoulders, short, wiry hair, and square jaw Sissy should have been named something less prissy and more, well, linebacker-y. Like Gertrude. Or Wilhelmina.

"Jason has all the characteristics of an only child, or 'super-first-born'." Jason's college-professor father rambled on in the background as he stared down the thick grasping fingers of his least favorite maiden aunt. A nun – Sissy would have made a great nun, he thought, having no trouble imagining Sister Sissy putting the fear of H – E – double hockey sticks into tiny children everywhere. But she'd taken care of Aunt Sarah for years and was fiercely protective of the fragile old woman, so Jason was willing to cut her a little bit of slack over the whole butt-pinching incident.

Inching his way sideways out of the line of fire, he hurried back towards the kitchen, carefully bypassing little pools of relatives as he walked down the wide hallway decorated with holly, pine boughs, and his mother's collection of nutcrackers. An unmistakable tenor voice oozed around the corner of his father's study. Uh-oh. Jason froze, the proverbial deer watching those fatal headlights come closer and closer.

"… but it's the perfect time, Nathan, you've got to jump on this volatile housing market – get them listed – they don't have to be perfect, just putty, patch, and paint. I've got the best stagers in the business. They can make a cracker-box look like an HGTV masterpiece. You can't be waiting around for tile from Italy or let the county catch up with you for permits…"

Ah, this is where Cousin Grant was hiding. He was determined to make his first million before age 30 and didn't mind sharing his Five Keys to Financial Success with anyone who slowed down long enough to get caught in his fun-sucking whirlpool. At Jason's high school graduation party, he had been backed into a corner by the man and subjected to a twenty-minute lecture, complete with visual aids by way of the PowerPoint App on Nathan's phone. Jason slid along the wall like a particularly stealthy ninja, hoping to ease past the open doorway before he was spotted.

Whew! Made it.

"Jason! We've been looking for you!"

Oh… Holy Night, he sighed, screwing up his eyes. Just when you thought it was safe to go into the kitchen. It was the triplets.

"Whatcha doin'?"

"Do you like our dress?"

"Did you see you're sitting next to us at dinner?"

Squinting one eye open, much like a soon to be eviscerated snowman place-card, Jason knew his goose was cooked. The three little girls looked to the unsuspecting, like perfect Christmas angels. Long blond hair, fancy silver dresses with different colored satin sashes, and the tenacity of bull terriers. And, apparently, while he'd been away, they had not found a new object of their stalking - er – affectionate attention.

"Hi Staci. Traci. Lacey." Was there some kind of naming curse that ran in his family? "You girls look nice."

They preened. They posed. They chattered like little feral chipmunks. Jason threw a glare at his mother's unsuspecting back. The kids' table. Maybe next year he'd take his roommate up on his invitation to spend Christmas with his crazy family. What was it his dad always said? 'A change was as good as a rest.' Well, he was certainly willing to give it a try.

After the usual adjustments, the strategic placement of chairs, the perennial grumbling of Grandpa Eddie, and one more plea to Uncle Dan to leave his perch in front of yet another college bowl game on the television, everyone was finally seated. Jason had managed a quick sleight of hand while the other kids were distracted, and his own tattered snowman now sat firmly between Frankie and the youngest cousin, five-year-old Matthew, who could not have done anything bad enough this year to have earned a place at Frankie's side. Across the table, the triplets frowned a moment at the unexpected change in position, but Jason only looked down crossly at the snowman, silently warning it to keep its mouth shut.

The kids had been allowed to fill their plates first, but Jason was kept busy, hopping up and down to fetch something that one of them had forgotten, or hadn't had room on his plate for the first time around.

It was strange, constantly traveling that no-man's-land between the kids' table and the adults', especially after the first face-stuffing silence gave way to semi-sated conversation again. Jason listened, considering.

"I know the fix was in on that one, Danny, or Pittsburgh would never have lost to Cleveland. Cleveland! Seriously!"

"Last weekend we made snow angels all along the front walk and mommy made hot chocolate for after. I love snow!"

"But with the volatile nature of Chinese imports right now, the Consumer Price Index is pretty useless."

"And I asked Santa for Legos. The new Harry Potter set. It's huge!" Matthew's grin wobbled. "Will you help me, Jason? Mommy says it might be hard for me."

"Sure thing, runt," Jason answered as he headed back to the big table for another bowl of cranberry sauce.

Uncle George was shouting. "What's in this, Annie? It's after six, and what with the diabetes and the high blood pressure, I gotta be careful or I'm gonna spend the rest of the night in the…"

Jason moved off hurriedly, juggling the cranberries and a basket of warm rolls, and quietly reciting the words to The Twelve Days of Christmas under his breath to block out whatever came out of his uncle's mouth next. He glanced out the dining-room window during his escape and noticed that the first flakes of snow were just beginning to cover the ground. Wow. Nice. How often did that happen? Snow on Christmas?

Smiling, he plunked down in his seat and turned to his young cousin. "What else did you get from Santa, Matthew?"

From his other side, Cowboy Frankie snorted. "C'mon, Jase, you know -"

A well-placed kick under the table sent Frankie howling and Jason turned back to the wide-eyed child sitting to his left. "Matthew?"

"I got this really cool Transformers helmet – it makes my voice sound just like Bumblebee, and it looks like him, and plays stuff from the movie and everything!" Matthew gushed. "And a new sled. I hope it snows; Daddy said it might. He said he could work from home, and we could go to the big hill at the park if it snowed."

Lacey – or maybe Traci – bounced in her seat. "Yeah, my Dad said the same thing. It would be like another Christmas present! Jason, is it gonna snow?"

"Did it snow when Jesus was born, Jason?" Another triplet asked, frowning. "The preacher didn't say."

Jason frowned. "Good question. I'm not sure how much snow

Bethlehem gets." He reached for the phone in his back pocket and then stopped. All eyes were fixed on him as if he held the secrets of the universe. "Um, the shepherds were out with their sheep, right? The flocks were grazing and, I'm pretty sure they wouldn't be able to do that if there had been snow."

"And the stars were bright, 'member?" Matthew nodded.

"That's true," Staci agreed. "And the angels came to sing, and nobody said anything about not being able to see them because of a blizzard."

"The roads weren't closed."

Jason turned, eyebrows rising, to stare at Frankie's not-snotty, not-snide tone of voice.

"Momma says just a little snow makes the roads bad. And, well," Frankie shrugged, "the kings got there from far, far away. On camels. I think that would be pretty hard in the snow."

"I think you're right," Jason found himself agreeing.

Matthew rubbed his nose with the back of one hand. "Still. It would be nice. I think baby Jesus would have liked some snow." His eyes were worried. "He only got three presents. Snow would be like a special one, from his Daddy up in heaven."

Something warm glowed in Jason's chest. Maybe it was just the jalapenos in his mother's cornbread, but Jason suddenly had a great idea. "I don't know about Bethlehem, but I heard it might snow here." He leaned low over the table and whispered. "Maybe we should go look."

Lacey glanced over towards the adult table where her father's

44

face was red from his enthusiastic defense of his golf hero. "Can we?"

"Can we, Jason?"

Weird. Where did the Terrifying Triplets, the Bronco Bully, and the hyped-up munchkin go? With just one little promise of a peek into the yard on the off chance of snow, the kids Jason had happily resented had turned into little people. What was up with that?

"Okay, but let's try to be quiet," he whispered.

The kids scrambled quickly from their seats and Jason looked down to find that Matthew had slipped one hand into his.

Straightening, he put one finger over his lips and led the little troop into the shadowy family room. The lamps had been turned off by eco-conscious Aunt Mickey and the room was lit by just the colored bulbs on the Christmas tree and the orange glow of the dying fire, adding a touch of mystery to the familiar furnishings. Jason noticed a thrill of anticipation beginning to creep up his own spine. Huh. Maybe he belonged at the kids' table after all. This was a lot more fun than fielding questions about his college life or fending off Grandpa Eddie's gall bladder stories.

The heavy curtains over the wide bay window hung silently, as if they were hiding a deep dark secret. Frankie and the triplets climbed up on the couch and propped themselves over the back, waiting, and Jason plucked Matthew up and perched him alongside the others before reaching for the curtains' cord.

"Oh, look!"

Big fat flakes dropped from the sky, a blanket of white covering the cars parked up and down the driveway and frosting the pine trees along the edge of the yard. Feeling like a stage magician, Jason gestured with one arm at the glittering scene and turned back to his audience.

Eyes big, the five children sat transfixed, faces pressed closer and closer to the glass until their breath misted its surface. The silent tableau held for a moment before Traci slipped from her spot and ran towards the dining room.

"Daddy, Daddy! It's snowing! Come and see!"

Jason stepped back as a few of the adults crowded around, the little girl merrily tugging her father towards her discovery.

"Oh, great. Just what we needed."

"Gonna be a nightmare trying to get home in this."

As the men and women slowly made their way back to the dining room, Jason stood quietly in the corner by the tree, watching. Watching the happiness of the children, listening to the grumbling of the adults, and wondering why he'd wanted to sit at the adults' table so badly anyway.

These kids could teach their parents a thing or two about appreciating Christmas. About being thankful. About what was really important. Not snow, or presents, he thought to himself, but Christmas miracles, a baby in a manger, and, especially, joy. Joy in all the little things.

"Then children were brought to him that he might lay his hands on them and pray. The disciples rebuked the people, but Jesus said, "Let the little children come to me and do not hinder them, for to

46

such belongs the kingdom of heaven." And he laid his hands on them and went away." Matthew 19:13-15

Frankie glanced over his shoulder and noticed Jason there. "Hey, Jase, remember when I creamed you in the face with a snowball last year?" He chortled and turned back to stare at the wintry sight.

Jason felt his mouth crook up into a half-smile. Yep. The kids' table was still better.

# I WISH YOU LIGHT

*I wrote this poem in 1978. A young Christian, trapped at home after my first year away at college where I had found my first chance of independence and fellowship. I missed my group of Christian mentors and friends from the Indiana University of Pennsylvania Inter-Varsity Fellowship chapter. I felt alone, abandoned back in my childhood bedroom, with only my difficult parents for company.*

*While I laid on my bed and listened to music, I wished. I wished for love. For light. For peace. And I realized others in much different, much worse situations, must wish the same. May you find the true Light this Christmas.*

I wish you light to guide your way,

When days are dark, and life is grey.

I wish you hope when all is lost,

And warmth to melt the winter's frost.


I wish you love when you're alone

And always harbor in the storm.


But most of all, I wish you peace,

That life's confusions daily cease,

That time is left for Lord and prayer,

That the Father keep you in His care.

# THE FOUR SUNDAYS OF ADVENT

*Advent wreaths and advent candles were a part of my childhood. Three purple candles, one pink, represented the four Sundays of Advent in the weeks before Christmas. Each Sunday was dedicated to a different aspect of devotion, celebrated, sometimes in different arrangements, in churches all over the world.*

*Hope. Faith. Joy. Peace.*

*Hope takes us back to the promises God made to his people in the Old Testament. To the prophecies about the Savior's birth, and the bright expectation of the Messiah. Faith is our response. The response of God's people to John the Baptist's announcement of His imminent birth. A reminder of our duty to prepare the way and pass on that announcement to others.*

*Joy is Mary's inspired prayer praising and glorifying the God who remembered his promises. And, finally, peace is the beyond-comprehension feeling in our gut that all the crazy, chaotic, dark, disturbing events around us still result in Jesus' victory over death.*

First Sunday of Advent. Hope.

Jeremiah 33:14-16 "Behold, the days are coming, declares the Lord, when I will fulfill the promise I have made to the house of Israel and the house of Judah. In those days and at that time I will

49

cause a righteous Branch to spring up for David, and he shall execute justice and righteousness in the land. In those days Judah will be saved, and Jerusalem will dwell securely. And this is the name by which it will be called: The Lord is our righteousness."

Pastor Jim knocked twice on the red church door. A silly habit. He rubbed his fingers along the faded paint. His tradition of 'touching wood' had rubbed this one spot nearly bare. He turned the key in the lock, shoulders hunched up around his ears.

"Where's your hat?"

He slipped his hand around his wife's waist. "I think I left it at Lois's house."

Rose tipped her head back to meet his eyes. "You have to be careful with that head. Especially at this time of year."

Jim brushed one gloved hand across his bare scalp. "You're right. I lost my natural insulation years ago," he chuckled. He tucked Rose in close, her head against his shoulder. "It's just an excuse to keep you closer to keep me warm, my dear."

They stepped down the shallow stairs to the sidewalk. "The season's just started." She sighed. "I should pull your warmer clothes from the wardrobe."

Jim pressed his lips against her hair. "I'll be fine. We've weathered how many advent seasons together now?"

"Forty-three, as if you don't know."

"Forty-five if you count before we were married."

Rose hummed in agreement. "Leah has been making soup all day."

Jim's mouth watered at the thought. Their middle daughter had inherited her French grandmother's culinary skills. With evening service to prepare for, Jim rarely had time for supper on Sundays. "I'm looking forward to that." His steps quickened, hurrying to the car.

He handed Rose into the passenger seat, tastebuds readying themselves for dinner and his stomach growling loud enough to make his wife chuckle. A voice behind him interrupted his thoughts.

"Pastor, Pastor Wallace? No, it couldn't be."

Jim turned. "Yes, I'm Pastor Wallace."

The lady standing before him certainly agreed with Rose about wearing layers. Two cardigans peeked out from inside her threadbare coat and pink knitted gloves covered her nervous fingers. Grey curls framed a weathered face beneath a green and purple stocking cap bearing an impressive bobble on top.

"Oh, no. You're much too young." The lady shook her head. "Pastor Wallace was not a wink younger than me. And not half so tall as you." She looked him up and down. "But you've got the look of him around the eyes."

Jim took the lady's hands in his. "You must mean my father, Pastor John Wallace. I'm afraid he passed into glory two years ago." The ache in Jim's chest would never go away.

"Oh, that's a pity." The lady clucked her tongue.

"And you are?"

"Iris. Iris Jones. You might remember –"

"Mrs. Jones. Of course, I remember you." Jim smiled. "Father spoke about you often. How you helped him at his first church in the

Hollow."

"Down the Hollow, yes." she corrected him automatically. "He was a good man, only needed a poke here and there, a word in his ear. Never seemed to resent it at all when I pointed him to those who really needed his help."

Jim tightened his grip on her hands for a moment. "Not at all. He mentioned how grateful he was to have someone like you to guide him. To tell him the stories of the folks who lived there."

Mrs. Jones shivered. "Saw your name on this pretty little church and had to stop," she murmured. "Ah, well, don't let me keep you."

Jim tilted his head, his memories churning. The Hollow was only about two dozen miles away, but the thought of it dredged up feelings of fabled forests and fairy tales. Of a time and place so different, so removed from their comfortable suburban sprawl that Jim could barely fathom it. Jim's father's first church. He had no idea it still stood.

Pastors' kids were used to moving. To leaving one church family behind and making others. Pastor John Wallace had found himself in many states and towns, serving small and large churches, or working as a teacher at various universities. When this old church building had gone up for sale ten years ago, Jim's father had considered it a blessing from God for his final days. Like coming home.

"Do you live in town, Mrs. Jones?"

"Oh, no," she waved one hand in dismissal. "Down the Hollow, born and bred. Don't know anything else. Don't want to. I was in town to pick up some boxes at the food pantry. Folks out west are feeling the crunch this year something awful. Some canned and dry goods will be welcome. Then, driving back, I got a bit turned around and, well, here I am. With a trunk full of food and a car that won't start. Decided to walk down the street to see if any folks were around to help and there I saw the name Wallace on the church sign, big as life."

Rose, listening quietly from behind him, spoke up. "That sounds like the hand of Providence at work, doesn't it?"

Jim drew her to his side. "This is my wife, Rose. Rose, Iris Jones, from down the Hollow."

Rose shook the lady's hand. "Is your car safe? Not stalled on a street somewhere?"

Mrs. Jones pointed to a dull silver sedan, bigger and boxier than the sleek, streamlined cars of today. It sat crookedly at the curb beneath a streetlight. "Seems so."

"Let's just transfer your goods to our car and you can come on home for a bowl of soup while we call for help."

Rose already had their car's back door open, gently herding the protesting woman into the seat. She handed Mrs. Jones' car keys to Jim and shooed him over to rescue the groceries.

After soup and bread, a little laughter, prayer, and warm memories shared around the table, Jim followed Iris west. Stu, one of the car guys from the church, had come around and fixed her up, but Jim and Rose didn't want to take any chances that Iris would run into trouble driving home tonight.

Hearing Iris talk about Jim's father's church had touched

something deep inside. Long before Jim was born, his father had lived and worked beside the people down the Hollow. People who knew only poverty and want but lived as joyously as anyone gifted with every creature comfort.

As he drove away from the townhouses, the larger homes on the outskirts of the city, and then the country farms still holding out against the suburban sprawl, Jim sighed. It was only an hour drive. Especially on a Sunday night. Yet the last time he'd been out this way was with his father the week they'd moved back to town.

The very first week.

His father had not hesitated to return to the people who had taught him what it meant to be a pastor. Beyond his divinity degrees, beyond the years he'd spent in high office of a large church, the people down the Hollow had taught John Wallace how to love others. How to care – to care for each person the way he or she needed to be cared for. To truly be a part, a vital member, of this small branch of the family of God.

Rose had been concerned about him driving back and forth after a busy Sunday. Worried about him. Jim smiled at Iris' taillights leading him along the winding country road. After spending little more than an hour with the lady, Jim felt more energized, more rested than he did after a day off with nothing to do.

The old church was still standing. Jim's headlights picked it out as he pulled into the gravel drive behind Iris. The wooden building leaned a bit, the window in the steeple had been boarded over. But someone had painted it recently. Bright white. The simple wooden church glowed in the quiet clearing: a welcome, a beam of invitation and encouragement.

Sitting and standing around the red-painted door, men and women and children were waiting. In the cold November night, they huddled close to a fire they'd lit in an old metal drum.

Jim swallowed in a throat thick with emotions. They must have been waiting for hours.

He pulled in next to Iris and popped his trunk. He couldn't make them wait an instant longer for what they needed.

When he opened the car door, the sound of singing broke over him. A Christmas carol. An old favorite, voices raised in joyful expectation of Emmanuel's promised appearance.

No one swarmed the cars. No one complained about their lateness or raised an angry rant. When the song was over, a few men approached Iris' car.

"Worried about you, Miz Jones."

"Thought we ought to send someone out looking."

"You okay, Ma'am?"

Iris waved her pink-mittened hands. "Just look what God provided."

She wasn't talking about the boxes of food in her trunk.

"Sir."

"Pastor."

"You look like your father."

"How's Pastor John? Haven't seen him for a long while."

Jim shook hands. Introduced himself. Learned the names of the families who came forward. He told them about his father's passing. Apologized for not coming sooner.

Still, no one grabbed at the boxes and parcels.

"You got a message for us, Pastor?"

Head bowed, Jim swallowed regret and apologies. He sent up a prayer. "Help me to serve them, Oh Lord."

Jim made his way to the stone steps leading up to the church door. He touched the bright, red paint, glossy and new, then turned to face the people. His people. His family.

"God is good," he murmured, encouraged by the warmth in his heart.

"All the time," one of the children answered.

He hadn't heard the call and response for decades. He grinned. "Tonight, you waited in expectation. Because you believed in Iris. In her promises. Thousands of years ago, others waited. Expecting a savior. Because they believed in God's promises. And, one cold night, in a dark stable, Jesus was born."

"Amen."

"Sure was."

"Better than a box of instant taters."

The crowd laughed.

"God kept his promises. And he always will," Jim said. "In a dark night, we have the light of Jesus Christ to warm our hearts. The warmth of friendship and fellowship. I'm grateful. Grateful to God, grateful to Mrs. Jones, and grateful to you all. For your faith through dark and lean times. For reminding me that my family doesn't end at my front door. That I have brothers and sisters here, just like my father did long years ago. Keeping the light burning. Faithfully waiting for God's promises."

"Still here." Mrs. Jones nodded briskly.

Still here. Jim took in the faces raised toward him. These men and women, brothers, and sisters, still faithfully waited. For help. For blessings. He smiled. For a box of instant potatoes and a word from God. He lifted his hands. Said a prayer. After the lingering Amen, he helped lift the boxes of food and supplies from his trunk.

As he drove home, his trunk empty, but his heart so full, Jim set the radio to play Christmas carols.

A family reunion, that's what it had been. Jim hadn't been the gift today, the people down the Hollow had been God's gift to him.


Second Sunday of Advent: Faith

> Isaiah 40:3 "A voice cries
> in the wilderness
> prepare the way of the Lord,
> make straight in the desert
> a highway for our God."


"Dad?"

Jim straightened, stretching his back from the hunched position he'd been in for too long.

"Lizzie! Where did you come from?" He caught the blur of blonde hair and bright blue puffy coat in his arms, steadying them both when the icy sidewalk threatened to throw them down. He held his youngest daughter at arms' length. "I thought you had swim practice this morning?"

She shook her head, the tiny icicles that had formed in her hair breaking and flying away in glittery rain. "Done. We can't practice as long on a Saturday. Too many kids swimming classes."

Jim raised his eyebrows. "And you walked all the way here from the pool?" Three miles at least, he figured. No wonder her nose was red. And running. "Come on."

Jim curled an arm around her shoulders and pushed the church door open.

"Is the heat on?"

She knew his routine too well. "I turned it up when I got here this morning, so you'll have to sit close to the floor units." It took forever to heat the high-ceilinged little church, so either Jim or one of his parishioners turned it up from 60 to 75 on Saturday mornings to get ready for Sunday.

Liz hurried ahead of him and plunked down on the floor in the right-hand aisle next to the heater. One knee bent, she picked at a frayed tear on her jeans.

"Hey. Did you hurt yourself?" Jim tugged off his thick gloves.

"The sidewalks are awful. I almost fell about ten times. Only managed to really go down once, though." She grimaced. "Mom's not going to be happy."

Jim spread the tear in the jeans wider, relieved to find a bump but no blood. "Not as unhappy as she would be if you truly hurt yourself. Why didn't you call for a ride?"

"No way," Liz frowned. "Mom had enough trouble on the

roads driving me to the pool."

Jim perched on the end of the pew, frowning. His fourteen-year-old daughter was safe walking through the town, he knew that. Still, he worried.

"And I knew you'd be here taking care of the sidewalk just in case anyone dares to drive over tomorrow," she shrugged.

"Some will come. Some always come, sweetheart."

Liz sighed. "I know. I just wish …"

"What?" he asked kindly.

"A lot of things, actually. That you had someone to take care of this for you. That we could hire someone like other churches do. That more people would come so your work wasn't wasted." Liz looked up at him, her eyes bright.

His daughter's wishes were nothing new. Nothing he and his family and his small congregation hadn't prayed for year after year.

"Have you invited anyone this week, Lizzie?"

"Dad?"

Jim chuckled. "All the prayer – all the wishing – in the world won't fill this church until we do our part. Have you done yours?"

"I have. You know that."

He hummed agreement. "Last summer, you brought a few friends. I enjoyed meeting them. Have you invited anyone lately?"

Liz made a face. "They all know, Dad. They all know my father is a pastor. It's not like they don't all see the church sitting here on the corner with your name on the sign. If they wanted to come …"

"'How then can they call on the one they have not believed in?

And how can they believe in the one of whom they have not heard?'"

Jim let Paul's words fade away before he continued. "We live here, in this town, in this country, and we believe that everyone around us knows. That they have all met our Savior and know his story. At this time of year, especially, we see signs of his birth all over the place." He leaned down and brushed the wet hair from Liz's face. "We're wrong. The people we meet, on the street, in the shops, even at your school, they haven't been introduced to Jesus. Maybe they have some fond memories of a baby in a manger, but they don't know how He grew up, how He lived, what He said, and, most importantly, how He died and rose for them."

Chin on her bent knee, Lizzie sighed. "I know."

"I know you know." Jim smiled at her snort of amusement. "Following Jesus, obeying his Great Commission, what does that mean?"

Liz managed to imply the irritated eyeroll of a pastor's kid, rather than be blatantly disrespectful. "Go ye therefore into all the world and preach my gospel to everyone."

Jim stood. "It's not that complicated in our little town. It all boils down to one word. 'Come.'" He gestured towards the door. "I make sure the sidewalk and steps are safe. That the heat is on. You could say it by handing your friends one of our Christmas Eve flyers. Just that. Nothing more." He touched her chin. "Think about it."

Jim slid his gloves back on and opened the church door to finish chopping at the layer of ice on the sidewalk. He nearly stumbled at the sight that greeted him.

"Hey, Pastor."

"Jim."

"Pastor."

"Where did you three come from?" he asked, fists on his hips.

Two deputies were attacking the ice with metal shovels while Sheriff Colb Skiller supervised. He shook Jim's hand. "One of the perks of the Sheriff's Office being a block away. Not even the criminals are out today, Jim." He gestured. "Gotta keep these guys busy."

"And work off the donuts."

Colb made a face. "Stereotypes and slander, Jim. We prefer your Leah's scones, and you know it."

Jim shook his head. "I'm so grateful for your help."

"No problem at all. Just say a few prayers for us."

"I always do." He leaned in and murmured, "And I'll put a bug in Leah's ear about the scones."

Deputy Larkin whooped and attacked the ice with renewed vigor.

In no time at all, the sidewalk was cleared, and the city's truck had gone by, spreading salt crystals on the road as the weak sun peeked out. Jim led the three men into the church and back towards the kitchen where Liz was just pouring the hot chocolate she'd made into a thermal carafe.

A weight had been lifted from Jim's shoulders and he gave thanks for the faithful men. For God's timing. For his daughter and her ready mind and bright spirit.

"Hi Sheriff. Deputies." Liz took down three more mugs from the cabinet and wiped them with a towel. "Good thing I made a lot."

Jim remained quiet, letting the four chatter about the weather, the town's readiness for another winter storm, and the lack of confidence they all had in weathermen in general.

"What are you going to do if it sleets again tonight, Pastor?" Deputy Larkin wiped a sleeve across his mouth.

"Come that much earlier tomorrow," Jim answered easily.

He watched the churning emotions cross his daughter's face. The clearing of her blue eyes.

"Um," she began, her voice hesitant, "you know you all could come tomorrow. To church, I mean. If, if you're not busy." Her cheeks reddened.

"Sure, sure," Larkin muttered, "just call us your ice clearing crew."

"No, that's not – that's not what I mean."

Jim laid his hand on Liz's. "They know that, sweetheart."

Sheriff Skiller bumped shoulders with his embarrassed deputy. "Ignore him, Miz Wallace. And thank you. For the hot chocolate." He raised his empty mug. "And for the kind invitation. Might just take you up on that."

Jim locked the doors behind them and waved at the three uniformed men trudging down the street.

"See? That wasn't so hard, was it?"

Liz pressed against his side. "I guess we should come early tomorrow to make sure the sidewalk is clear. Because people need to come, to hear God's message."

"That's a good idea."


Third Sunday of Advent: Joy

Zephaniah 3:14-17 "Sing aloud, O daughter Zion!
    Shout, O Israel!
Rejoice and exult with all your heart,
    O daughter of Jerusalem!
The LORD has taken away the judgments against you
    he has cleared away your enemies;
the King of Israel, the LORD, is in your midst,
    you shall never again fear evil.
On that day, it shall be said to Jerusalem:
    Fear not, O Zion, let not your hands grow weak.
The LORD, your God, is in your midst,
    a mighty one who will save;
he will rejoice over you with gladness,
    he will quiet you by his love,
he will exult over you with loud singing."


Rose slipped into Jim's office just as he was fixing the purple stole around his neck. Her smile didn't slip, couldn't slip, while she adjusted it, smoothing the silk, adjusting the ends to hang perfectly equal.

Jim had the same silly smile on his own face with no hope at all of turning it into something more solemn and fitting for the worship service.

"Everyone's here," Rose said as she stepped back.

Jim caught her hands in his. "Yes. Now, everyone is here."

His wife's eyes shone. "I'm ..." She shook her head, tongue-tied.

Jim gathered her close, eyes closed, and whispered a prayer. "Dear Lord. How can we hope to thank you for this? For this gift? For this precious child you've given our family?"

The organ prelude sounded quicker, happier today than it ever had in Jim's memory. Childish laughter rang out from behind the thin wall. Lois' low, rumbling voice urged quiet. As Jim entered the sanctuary he paused, taking in the sight of his entire family sitting in pew three, piano side. Right where they belonged.

Three daughters, various shades of dark blonde leaning over each other. Rose, her silver hair braided like a crown around her head. One small dark head resting against his oldest daughter's chest, almond-shaped eyes wide as Jim moved to the front.

Songs rose to heaven; holy words were read. The familiar order of service moved on, a ritual, a routine that joined God's people together in the weekly Sabbath miracle. Expectation lifted the fine hairs on Jim's arms and quickened his heartbeat.

"Praise God from whom all true blessings flow." He lifted his hands, still grinning, as he called the elders forward. "Today it is my joy, my grateful joy to present this family with its newest child."

Lois whispered in her new daughter's ear, lifting the small one-year old to rest on one hip. She joined Jim in front, her sisters and mother spreading out behind her.

Jim met the sparkling gazes of his congregation.

"Today, we celebrate this covenant child with the sacrament of Baptism. But, more than that, today we each remember and acknowledge our own adoption into the body of Christ. All of us, bearing every color of skin, hair that is red or brown, curly, or straight, or," he rubbed his hand on his bald head, "a shade that no one quite remembers. Our faces, our eyes, our noses, all different shapes. Speaking in languages and accents that may sound foreign. With distinct cultures and traditions."

He gestured towards the stained-glass windows. "Worshipping in churches across town and across the country and across the world, believers have been adopted into one church, one family. Just as our new granddaughter, Lily Anne Wallace, has been adopted by Lois, our daughter."

The usually controlled, reticent congregation exploded with loud applause, laughter, and shouts of joy.

Lily turned her face into Lois' neck and hid. Lois, one hand on her daughter's back, didn't bother to hide her tears.

"An unexpected, longed-for, dearly loved child has come to us." Jim folded his hands together, gripping tight. "We are blessed to welcome her. And I find myself, like Zechariah, speechless."

"Not quite," one of the elders beside Jim muttered.

"Okay, not quite." More laughter greeted him. "I can only rejoice. Shout out my thanks and gratitude to our heavenly Father. Not just for Lily Anne, but for all of us. All of my brothers and sisters, adopted into one family of God. I pray our family will grow in love, in encouragement, in grace as little Lily grows in the wisdom and admonition of the Lord."

The words of baptism flowed. Lily made a face as he sprinkled water on her head. Lois answered the traditional questions, her voice strong, and the family of God stood and welcomed Lily with promises of acceptance and guidance.

Jim knew he could count on them. Lily may have been born in a foreign land, abandoned by her mother, raised in poverty and want, but, among her spiritual family, she would never want for big brothers and sisters. Aunts and uncles. Grandparents.

That's how the church worked. How it should work. All adoptees together in their Father's family.

A child had been born into the family. In more ways than one.


Fourth Sunday of Advent: Peace

Isaiah 9:6 "For to us a child is born, to us a son is given: and the government shall be upon his shoulder: and his name shall be called Wonderful Counsellor, Mighty God, Everlasting Father, Prince of Peace."


Peace. Apparently, it looked a lot like chaos. Like mess, strewn wrapping paper, spilled coffee, and a cat knocking chess pieces off the board just because he could.

Later, peace sounded like fierce arguments about Park Place and Professor Plum. Teasing over whether or not to desecrate the pecan pie with ice cream rather than the familiar sprayed whipped topping. A blond girl racing down the hallway chasing a cat carrying off his prey of a bacon-wrapped shrimp.

Peace was a chilly car packed tight with warm bodies and a fussy child for over an hour.

Peace smelled like a musty old church and burnt coffee in old metal urns.

No gracious organ music rose to fill the rafters. No drift of pure snow smoothed the rough edges and rust on the cars and trucks pulled up outside. No bright stars lit the silent night, not with the new freeway built too close or the thickening grey clouds.

Still, peace reigned.

Peace filled the gathered hearts, soothed fears, and shoved worries and cares out of the way so that gratitude and joy could bloom.

Together, Iris Jones and her friends raised familiar songs. Rose and her daughters – and grand-daughter – served plates of food, played with children, helped older worshippers find the most comfortable chairs.

Pastor Jim regarded his family, built of blood and spirit and adoption. "Give thanks to the Lord for He is good," he whispered.

The peace of God felt like love. The love of a Father for his Son. The love of a new mother for her miraculous child. The love of the Son for all of his stubborn, ridiculous followers. The love of the best kind of family, warts and worries and all.

# CHRISTMAS 2020

*2020. It was another year of loss, of grief, of despair. This time, the loss was felt not just in our church, but all over the world. We were distanced from one another. Some were fearful. Many died. Children and parents were anxious, teachers and medical workers overtaxed. Some were angry at the loss of control over their lives.*

*And yet, the church remained the church. Whether we met together physically or by means of shared electronics, the church stood. No matter our reaction, God's people strived to love Him and our neighbors. Still, many felt at a loss, wondering whether or not we could possibly make a difference.*

*As if God's rich love and mercy could be diminished by trial.*

*Thank you, family of God, for your love, your gentleness, your honesty, and your steadfastness. You did make a difference.*

The organ keys danced under his fingers, his slippered feet dodging from one pedal to another. Frank smiled, the carol's majestic notes so familiar and so welcome in the empty church. The music rushed from the pipes, eager to spread, to rise up into the belfry, to slide along the cracked plaster walls and in and out of the pews as if looking for listening ears.

It wouldn't find any but Frank's. Not today. Not for months, now. Later, when Pastor Jim arrived, he'd set up the sound and the camera to send the music and message of Christmas Eve out along unseen wavelengths to screens and phones around the world. The Christmas story would reach many more ears than if the church were filled to the brim with worshippers, he reminded himself. But still ...

Frank started again, this time, singing along under his breath.

"On Christmas night, all Christians sing
To hear the news the angels bring.
On Christmas night, all Christians sing
To hear the news the angels bring.

News of great joy, news of great mirth
News of our merciful King's —"

His feet slipped against a wide, furry obstacle and a long droning note marred the beautiful melody.

Frank lifted his hands from the keyboard and looked down at the wide green eyes staring up at him.

"Definitely off key, Vespers."

"Mrrrrt," the cat replied.

Chuckling, Frank shut down the organ, cutting off the bass pedals' droning. "Yes, I imagine that I've practiced enough." Somehow, filling the church with music eased his heart — even if there was no one to hear it. He glanced down at the church cat. "We're told to use our gifts, Vespers. What's yours again?"

The tabby lowered himself to meatloaf position, paws tucked

under, still balancing on two wooden pedals. His rumbling purr replaced the organ music with a tune of his own.

"That can't be comfortable." Frank shook his head. "To each his own." He shuffled his sheet music into the correct order on the stand, checking it one more time against the Order of Service he'd printed off earlier and then slid to the end of the bench.

"You miss them, too, don't you, my friend?" Frank kept up a running one-sided dialogue, filling in the tabby's part for him. "All the warm hands, the sneaked treats. Never enough, of course. Yes, yes, I know." He scratched the cat between the ears, Vespers' eyes closing as his purrs rumbled louder. "You don't miss the tail pulling or the too-tight hugs from the little ones." Frank leaned down to whisper. "But I bet you'd take them, too, tonight."

Frank stepped up to the pulpit, adjusting the glass of water, checking the ribbon bookmarks on the Bible against the passages Jim would read later. He checked the Bluetooth mike with his phone. "Testing. Testing. Now there were in the same country shepherds living out in the fields, keeping watch over their flock by night. And behold, an angel of the Lord stood before them, and the glory of the Lord shone around them, and they were greatly afraid." He switched off, replayed the recording, and deleted it.

When he glanced up, he paused, taking a moment to look out over the church from the singular vantage point.

Their church wasn't the biggest in town. Not the newest, perfectly proportioned for sound and light, strung with enough gadgets and gizmos to have weathered this Quarantine Year with ease. It wasn't the oldest, either, relying on classic architecture, cathedral ceilings, or flying buttresses to draw in those who valued gothic beauty. But it had a few things going for it.

The central aisle had made it popular with brides – back when there were grand weddings to celebrate. Frank sent up a rushed prayer of gratitude: thankfully, the other traditional usage of a central aisle had not been needed much this year, either.

The church's middling size wasn't intimidating in either direction. Not too imposing for simpler folk, and not too tiny for those who preferred to fade into the background. Visitors had always been welcome, some wandering in off the main street out of curiosity or serendipity or God's leading, he reminded himself. Some, he was grateful to say, responding to the music.

Peering through the dim candlelight, Frank noted movement near the doors. Speaking of visitors, there was someone in the vestibule.

Trotting down the three steps from the pulpit, Frank hurried down the aisle, snatching his mask from his vest pocket. He'd thrown open the doors before he'd begun to practice, as was his habit, hoping the sacred music would touch a lonely heart here, a desperate mind there. Speed through the town to fill up hollow spaces with light and love. It wasn't much, not when so many were hurting, but it was Frank's gift to give.

It seemed someone had followed the music home. Or, maybe, they'd just ducked in for some warmth.

"Hello. How can I help?" Frank offered before he'd traveled

halfway towards the door. He didn't want to startle the visitor. Didn't want it to seem like he was storming down to evict him from the premises.

The man was middle height if Frank could judge from the hunched posture and lowered head. He was clean, his dark hair combed, his light wool coat only frayed around the hem. Not homeless, then.

The man lifted his head, revealing a creased forehead and a pair of dull green eyes above his mask. He held a snow-studded stocking cap in both hands as if he were a poor boy begging for bread. His gaze traveled here and there around the empty church, taking in the lit candles, the green wreaths, red bows bright against dark wood.

"I heard the music ..."

Frank wished he could read expressions when half of the faces of those he met were hidden.

"I'm so glad," Frank began when it was clear that the man would not go on. He hoped his smile reached his eyes. "My playing isn't perfect, but I've always felt music was one of God's most generous gifts."

"Yes, me too." The man shrugged. "It always seemed to lift the darkness. Before."

"'Before?'" Frank prompted.

The man sighed, his gaze moving to Frank. "Before all this."

"Ah." Frank stepped back, hoping to lure the man to follow him. "Would you like to sit? Talk?" The season took its toll on the most even-tempered people. This year ... this year had stolen far more and had left thousands in a morass of hopelessness and dread. He couldn't help glancing over his shoulder, hoping Jim was close. Jim was the pastor: good with people, easy to talk to. Frank was too tall, too bulky, built like a linebacker and with the interpersonal skills to match.

"Not much to say," the man murmured. His movements revealed more than his words. He stepped inside, sliding into the last pew on the left. "Talking doesn't change anything."

"Depends on who you talk to." Frank slipped into the opposite pew on the right. "I'm Frank."

"David."

The silence filled the church as the music had moments ago. Frank let himself sink into the pew. There was no hurry. No schedule to keep, not on this particular Christmas Eve. He wouldn't be rushing to unlock the back doors for the ladies setting up their goodies, punch and cookies and the traditional Buche de Noel. The deacons wouldn't be early, setting candles and song-sheets in each pew. The Sunday School teachers would not be racing around to find lost costumes and props for the children's pageant, shepherding their charges like so many stubborn sheep.

Frank folded his hands in his lap, head bowed. 'Thank you, Father,' he sent upward. He could give David all the time that he needed tonight.

"Oh, hello."

Frank glanced up and chuckled. A certain rumbling purr should have warned him. Vespers leaped up onto David's knees, uncaring of his welcome.

"I'm sorry –" Frank began.

Behind the mask, David might be smiling. "No, it's no problem." He brushed his hand down the cat's wide back, stopping to scratch at the base of his tail that lifted happily. "He's a cat. He goes where he likes."

"I see you're a cat person." Dog people tended to pat.

"Definitely. Cats seem to have the right attitude." David readjusted his legs as Vespers wandered in a circle, and then another.

Frank hummed, noncommittal. Vespers was not exactly a paragon of Christian values.

After the cat had settled, David's petting seemed to also settle the man.

"Everything's changed," he whispered.

Before Frank could respond, the visitor continued. "I can't see my parents. They're in a care facility – my dad has Alzheimer's," David explained. "Even if they allowed it, I can't in good conscience carry anything in there."

Frank nodded.

"My sister is a nurse. My brother, an EMT."

Ah. Front-line workers limiting their contacts with others, just in case, Frank noted. He mentally added David's family to his prayer list.

"I live alone," David continued. "Work from home, now. I look forward to this night every year. Getting together with my family, doing the traditional Christmas time things with them. Picking out the tree, decorating, eating all my sister's cookies." He lifted his gaze from Vespers' pleased expression to the pulpit. "Christmas Eve service." He tapped his chest over his heart. "It sustains me when I'm … when I'm feeling like this. Knowing I'd see them. Celebrate with them."

"Yes, before you ask, I'm Zooming with them all later. We talk all the time. But it's not the same."

"It isn't," Frank agreed. "We're human beings. We crave contact. Closeness." He tapped his own chest in an echo of David's gesture. "Even card-carrying introverts are craving more this year."

David laid his hand flat on Vespers' back. "You're not going to tell me how lucky I am? How fortunate we are to live in a day and age where we have things like Zoom and the internet?"

Frank tilted his head. "Not feeling particularly lucky?"

David's snort was answer enough.

"If it's practical advice you're looking for, I'm afraid I am in short supply." Frank opened his hands. "We're each finding our own way through this. Some with more grace and joy than others – which is not a judgment on those who cannot find those attributes." He pressed his lips together. Pastor Jim would be so much better at this. 'Lord, help me not make this man's lot even worse,' he prayed. A thought came to him, something that David said. "I can offer this: not everything has changed."

Frank stood and invited David to follow him with a waving hand. Vespers grumped but hopped down to precede the two men out through the still open church doors, his tail waving like a drum major leading a parade.

Outside, lit by spotlights, the church's Nativity Set gleamed in the softly falling snow. Frank brushed Joseph's head clean then bent to do the same for Mary. The empty manger looked like it had acquired a soft white blanket. Vespers sat in the sheltered spot beneath the donkey's nose, tail curled around his paws.

Frank found words waiting to be spoken rise within him. "Beneath the surface, deeper than masks and distancing and fear, the important things remain unchanged. Love. Charity. Forgiveness. Help is given in times of need. Memories are clearer. Hearts are reminded to cherish those we love, to not waste a day." Frank nodded towards the nearly life-sized figures. "Wise men, like you, still seek Him. Men and women, poor and rich, empty of hope, look up to find the source of all hope." He turned to face his visitor. "And God still answers."

"Jesus still comes," Frank continued. "On Christmas Eve the world celebrates this greatest gift. But they forget that He comes every day. Every hour. That has never changed. And it never will."

"Tonight might be a little more 'silent,' more 'still' than we'd usually sing about in the old songs." Frank shrugged. "Somehow, that's a gift, too. Don't ask me to explain it, though."

David's eyes seemed brighter over his mask. "I guess I needed the reminder."

"I know it doesn't change your circumstances." Frank shook his head. Maybe his words had been too big and preachy. Telling a hurting man that God was with him, would always be with him, how could that be enough?

"Prayer often doesn't," David acknowledged. "That's what this was, my coming here. A prayer. I couldn't put it into words other than 'help, Lord.'"

Frank's heart swelled with gratitude. "That's the best prayer of all."

David rubbed his fingers across his eyes before meeting Frank's inquiring gaze again. "Thank you. For the music. For your open doors. For the reminder."

"I didn't –" Frank stopped, his tongue tied. The cat meowed, cold and mournful, and twined about his ankles. "I'm glad you came, David. Come any time."

Both men turned as, from down the block, another church organ's music rang out. The light from its steeple was joined by another across the street, and more across the hills.

Frank murmured the words of the song. "Unto us a Child is born. Unto us a Son is given. And his name shall be called Wonderful Counsellor, the Mighty God, the Everlasting Father, the Prince of Peace."

When he turned back, David had gone.

"Not sure I was much help," Frank muttered, leaning down to scratch the tabby between the ears. "What do you think, Vespers."

"The cat's name is Vespasian."

Frank turned to smile at his pastor. "And, for the hundredth time, that's a dumb name for a cat."

Pastor Jim's blue eyes gleamed with amusement. No, it was

more than that. It looked like joy. "I think you gave David exactly what he needed."

Frank huffed. "Could have used your help."

The pastor stood before the empty manger. "You had all the help you needed."

Later, sitting once again at the organ in the nearly empty church, camera and sound sending the music around the world, Frank murmured a prayer of gratitude to God. "Prayer works both ways," his pastor had reminded him. Maybe Frank had been the answer to David's prayer, and perhaps David had answered some need in Frank, as well. The need to reach out, to share God's word with a stranger. The need to help.

Some things hadn't changed at all.

# MY FATHER'S VOICE

*This last story was the first I wrote for my church. My testimony story. A story of faithfulness through trial and hope through despair. My sister is the hero of this story, and of my life. First born, stubborn, strong enough to weather my father's wrath and share the good news with her confused little sister.*

*Although many live devout lives, like my father, sing hymns and recite prayers, many miss the point. They don't hear God's message behind the words and music. I am grateful that the music of Christmas communicated God's love to me, and that He made sure it found its way into my rocky heart.*

It's Christmas Eve again and the house is quiet. I've left the tree lights on, white bulbs among the greenery. I'll turn them off, soon, when I head up to bed. But I'm not ready yet. The family long ago returned from Christmas Eve service, from hearing the Christmas story and singing all the beautiful carols. We laughed and hugged our friends, exchanged last minute gifts, and then bundled up for the trip home. A couple of turns around the neighborhoods to see the Christmas lights is our traditional way of wrapping up Christmas Eve.

My daughter is too old for Santa, so the days of me staying up late to "magic" the gifts out from hiding and under the tree are over. She's been too old and too wise for years, but my memories are heavy on my shoulders, so sleep won't be coming soon. Not for me.

Don't get the wrong idea. My memories aren't dark with regret or tearfully maudlin like so many popular Christmas movies. But they're here, present, tangible, too bright to let me close my eyes. My childhood self is here in the room with me, my older sister and brother sitting near the tree, mom and dad over there by the old Lester spinet. Even though I'm the mom now, my daughter nearly grown with Christmas traditions of her own, my heart is in the past, in that little house on Londonderry Drive, drifted around with piles of snow and wearing one single strand of colored lights along the eaves.

It's part of the Christmas magic. The scent of pine, the silent countryside, they sharpen my memories. This year, it's the Christmas music that drags me back to that little house; the music of the church, carols and melodies that are hauled out and dusted off at this time of the year. Especially that one song, my father's favorite. The one he practiced beside that old spinet, my mom's hands drifting across the keys. The one he sang every Christmas Eve in church from my earliest memories. I heard it on the radio tonight. And, suddenly, I'm back there, listening to my father's voice.

There was always song at home. Music playing, someone tinkering at the piano, or organ, or guitar, or recorder. Or, God help us, trumpet. And my father, very much the head, boss, chief, and sovereign of my family, dominated in every way, even musically. His voice soared, it echoed. A deep, rich bass, it overwhelmed every other sound.

In person, he was loud, volume set permanently at eleven. On the phone, you had to hold the receiver away from your ear to retain your hearing. But in song my father's voice was magnificent.

My mother played the piano for him when he practiced, and he practiced every day, learning the sacred music he sang in churches and choirs around the city. You couldn't help hearing him in every corner of that tiny house. I got to hear it most. I was the youngest, and so, the most housebound. While my 16-year-old brother had a car, such as it was, and a job, such as it was, and my 19-year-old sister was at college, I was stuck at home, listening again and again to my father's voice.

It was part of our home's landscape. Ugly nubby green couch, check. Harvest gold kitchen appliances, check. Weird horse/bird thing my brother made in woodshop on the shelf, check. My father singing, leaning over my mother's shoulder? Yes, that, too.

When you hear something repeated often enough it becomes a part of you. Multiplication tables. Star Trek quotes. The Lord's Prayer. In my home, the songs of the Christmas season were sung every year, over and over and OVER. Relentlessly. By the age of thirteen, I had every song memorized. Every verse, every voice's part, especially my father's. All those songs slid in through my ears and took root in my memory. I can't remember what happened to me last week, but, yes, I can sing all five verses of "We Three Kings of

Orient Are" perfectly to this day. Not very helpful unless you find yourself on Christmas Carol Jeopardy, but I will be your phone-a-friend if you ever need all the lyrics to "Good King Wenceslas."

As you can imagine, my father's voice was not always raised in song. It was raised in many other ways throughout my childhood. My brother's report card always brought about some added volume. Teaching each kid to drive was accompanied by a full range of vocal exercises. But there was another Christmas tradition that set my father to rare vocalizing: putting up the family Christmas tree.

No traditional, live Christmas tree for us, my family had a modern, aluminum tree, very much in style in the tradition-ignoring sixties and disco seventies. It came with a revolving tree stand that played Christmas carols, and a colored light wheel that made the tree appear blue, green, red, or yellow as it turned. Imagine the beauty.

Unfortunately, those who designed this tree were evil, sadistic men, as the correct placement of the branches depended on a system of colored dots painted on the end of each branch. As time wore on and the dots wore off, many hours of trial and error were spent by my father, crouched under the shiny silver branches. I learned many, um, colorful metaphors as Mister Spock would say, from my father's voice.

We had some great Christmas traditions, too. Our advent wreath, piles of Christmas cookies, eggnog, those paper luminaires that lined our neighbor's sidewalk. We had school Christmas plays — not Winter Holiday plays, mind you, real Christmas plays. We shopped for presents in actual stores with actual clerks exchanging actual dollars for merchandise, with the actual nasty mid-west weather threatening every move.

We had train sets. The black Lionel engine, the coal cars, and mail cars, pipe cars, and cars that carried cars. We even had a plastic gas station, and I would take the autos from the train and drive them all around the basement. Vrrroooom. The hum of the transformer and the smell of the ozone are indelible parts of my Christmas memories.

But Christmas time was, mostly, about song. Songs of the long-awaited birth of Jesus. Familiar carols, Christmas hymns, and special songs that our choir director handed to my father to start practicing sometime after Thanksgiving. Every year, every Christmas since I could remember, my father sang them all.

He sang carols and hymns with the choir, and I learned the bass parts better than the melody from listening to him practice. He traditionally sang one King's part in the carol, "We Three Kings." Unfortunately, the one written to the deepest voice was not a particularly cheerful verse: "Myrrh is mine its bitter perfume, breathes a life of gathering gloom. Sorrowing, sighing, bleeding, dying, sealed in a stone-cold tomb." Very festive!

My father concentrated intensely on his music, and, looking back on it, I realize that he sang beautifully. Technically perfect, with wonderful tone and timing. And yet, he totally missed the point. As I sat listening, all those days and nights, so did I.

I move to the window, gazing out on the thin layer of snow coating the cold ground like a blanket. It's so quiet. So still. Not like one particular Christmas that is etched into my memory.

On my thirteenth Christmas, the sounds of our home were harsh, and voices weren't raised in song, but in anger. My sister, a somewhat independent college student now, had heard the gospel of Jesus Christ as she never had during all of our Catholic upbringing. She'd brought her new insights home to share with excitement and wonder: words like grace and mercy, the sufficiency of God's Word, and the Lordship of our Savior. And she ran straight into the backlash of my father's reaction.

My sister was anxious to share the good news. Good news that shouldn't have been news to us, people raised in the church, in Catholic school, submerged in the lessons of the music. But, somehow, it was.

The days were filled with arguing and simmering anger, while my sister's nights were full of tears and prayers. And then came the threats. The message of grace and salvation was silenced. My sister was told that if she tried to "preach" to us – to me in particular, the youngest, the baby - she would be thrown out of the house and cut off from the family. And so, she despaired of ever reaching us with Christ's message of grace.

At Christmas. At the celebration of the Savior's arrival. The irony is not lost on me.

As a young teenager, my own thoughts and feelings were confused and anxious. I missed most of the worst arguments, hearing only part of the story. The part that meant turmoil every day, knots in my stomach, and a feeling of helplessness. The songs of the season were lost to me; they were just background noise to the more immediate sounds my family was making. My father was deep in rehearsal for the season's music, but the words were now sung with an undercurrent of rage that made me sad.

Still. I had heard the hymns and carols hundreds of times before, and I felt better for their familiarity. These traditions were comforting. They let me believe that everything would be okay. That my familiar life would not be destroyed, and our family broken.

I hung on to those traditions with both hands. I watched the silvery tree glow, I shopped, I helped mom bake. I gladly went to church, knowing that nothing new would ever happen there, that each service was exactly like the one before, with the customary prayers and responses. It was a relief to know I wouldn't have to think, or feel, or even pay attention at church.

But dread lay like a ball of uncooked dough in my stomach. I waited, Christmas approaching, anticipating the explosion.

Finally, it was Christmas Eve. My father had practiced his special song for church, my brother had finished wrapping last minute purchases, and my mother was putting dinner in the oven. For some reason, my parents decided we would open our presents on Christmas Eve, before the traditional midnight Mass, instead of waiting until Christmas morning. Maybe they felt that this would bring a spirit of love and peace to our Christmas that year, or maybe they were just exhausted: tired of preparing for that perfect Christmas that everyone longs for, that never quite arrives. Especially not this year, not at our house.

Down to the Rec Room we went, a Christmas 8-track playing, the silver tree glistening. I remember opening a record album from my brother, and a stereo from my parents, and other items from distant relations. But then I received something I did not expect. My sister handed me a package. It was obviously a book, and since I read every book I could get my hands on, I was excited. Then she handed an identical package to my brother, who hadn't read anything but motorcycle magazines in years, and one to my parents. Her eyes were filled with worry, her hands trembling. She was afraid. But, squaring her shoulders, my sister met my father's scathing glare and did not falter.

Carefully unfolding the wrapping paper, I discovered that my sister had given each of us a Bible.

A Bible? I had never had one, except the Children's Story Bible my godmother had given me on my First Communion. At first, I felt disappointed. It wasn't a story, not mystery or science fiction. But then I looked at my sister and saw the joy and fear on her face as she waited for my response. I smiled. She loved me, and she'd braved my father's wrathful voice to give me something from her heart.

I turned at my mother's anxious whisper to see her clutching my father's arm with one hand. His face wore an expression of tightly clenched fury. "It's a Living Bible," my mother was saying. "Look. It's okay."

The Living Bible was one of only a few translations that, as Catholics, we were permitted to read. My father ground his teeth and, with only a few dark comments rather than an angry tirade, settled back in his chair. The storm clouds weren't gone, but they were quiet, for the moment. and I could breathe again.

After the final package was opened that night, my sister came to my side.

"What do you think?" she asked me.

My hands flipping through the pages, I shrugged my shoulders. "I don't know where to start," I whispered back.

She stilled my nervous fingers and opened the Bible to the Book of Luke. "Try here. You'll recognize this story." Her eyes were kind as she continued. "God wrote this," she murmured. "He's been writing it since the beginning of time. It's a story, and He's proud of it. He wants to share it with you."

Something in my heart whispered that this gift was different from any I'd received before.

I headed to the bedroom I shared with my sister and plunked myself down on my bed and began to read. She was right; I knew this story. I'd heard it over and over again from the lips of our priests, from carols, even from Linus on A Charlie Brown Christmas. I found that the songs my father sang were in there, too. The Magnificat, the song of joy that Mary sings, was there. The heralding of Emmanuel was there. The visit from the Kings was there. They were all there, in this book, this story that God had written to me, and I had never really heard them.

"Pay attention," said something within my heart. "Listen to your Father's voice."

Later, shuffling into our familiar pew at Midnight Mass, nothing appeared to have changed. We'd ridden there in a familiar strained silence, saw the same familiar sights along the way, and looked up at the familiar view of our father up in the choir loft above the altar. The incense stung our eyes and set my brother to sneezing. The parishioners were dressed up, jewelry glittering, new coats and hats and gloves in abundance.

But then, something different happened. It wasn't the smell of too much perfume, or the glow of the candles. It wasn't the priests' shining vestments, or the heavy solemnity in the air. The majestic pipe organ was silent as the voices of the choir, my father's voice leading, rose, unaccompanied and pure. The words were the same as they had always been, the choir singing softly, beginning as a murmur, so quiet that I must strain to hear:

"Let all mortal flesh keep silence, as with fear and trembling stand. Ponder nothing earthly minded, but with blessings in His hand Christ our God to earth descendeth, our full homage to demand."

As the sound of the first verse of the familiar hymn died away into the silence of the full church, it was the Holy Spirit who spoke within me, "Listen with your heart."

That Christmas Eve, I began to understand what my father and mother never had: that the music and the singing were not the goal, that perfection of pitch and rhythm was not the highest aspiration of the season. No, my father's clear, steady voice, his "performance" was not the purpose of Christmas, the ends, if you will, it was the means. The means given to my father by God so that he could lead others to rejoice. In the words of the hymn, that we might pay our full homage to Him.

The Christmas music came alive for me that night as it never had before. I found the love of God revealed in the words of the Bible, and the deep faith of the composers in the music. I heard my father, even in his anger and confusion, striving to give something back to God with the gifts he had received. The music hadn't changed, the words were certainly familiar, but everything was different. Tonight, I was listening to the sounds of hearts set free from bondage, hearts of joyful gratitude for the precious Christmas gift of Jesus Christ.

We sank back into the pew as the lights grew dim. It was time for my father's solo, a song that I had heard him sing many, many times before. I knew every word, and every note. I knew my mom was listening for perfection, for clear notes and proper timing. I knew my brother wasn't really listening at all. I looked at my sister and squeezed her hand, trying to tell her, to share without words, that, for the first time, I heard.

"O come let us adore Him, O come let us adore Him, O come let us adore Him, Christ the Lord."

Compared with the perfect gift of the Savior, the pains and trials of my family seemed small and unimportant. They'd still be there when I returned home that Christmas morning. My mom would not turn into June Cleaver, my brother wouldn't immediately become kind and considerate of my feelings, my father would not decide to stop yelling, and my sister, wanting so much to share her joy, would still be bound by his rules. But these troubles were overshadowed, for a moment, by the joy of hundreds of voices raised in song, and the memories of millions who came before, joining from heaven in worship and praise.

I laid the afghan on the couch and hesitated at the doorway, my hand on the light switch. The green, fresh scent of the tree fills the room, the peace of the angel on top drifting down through the silence. I was hundreds of miles from the cold and slush of my childhood home, and many, many years away from my thirteenth birthday. Beneath my breast I could still feel that first bright joy I felt that night. The sudden spark of the Christmas star in my heart.

I thanked God for his gift of Jesus Christ, for his Word, and for my sister who was brave enough and loving enough to share them with me. Where would I be now, I wonder, if God hadn't sent her to me that night with a Bible in her hand? And where would I be if God hadn't planted all those seeds in me beforehand through the songs of the season and my father's voice.

Mom and dad are gone, now. My sister and brother far away. But tonight, looking up at the clear winter sky, I know my sister and I are joined by something no distance can measure. By our love, by God's grace, by our memories, good and bad. By music and singing and laughter and tears. By sparkling silver trees and 8-track carols. She's attending her own church services, playing the piano so that the congregation can fill the air with their worship and gratitude. This year, every year, just as she taught me, she's listening with her heart.

I turned off the lights. Low and sweet, so that my voice didn't wake my family sleeping upstairs, I sang. "O come let us adore Him,

Christ the Lord."

# ABOUT THE AUTHOR

Maryel Stone is a native Pittsburgher and retired High School English and Literature teacher. Raised Catholic, nurtured in IVCF in college, and taught catechism by her Reformed pastor, her Christian walk has been sharpened in many denominations and church communities over the years. Each one played a unique role in her spiritual journey, and she's grateful for the love and training she received along the way.

Living in Virginia, Maryel spends her time visiting wineries with her husband, cat-sitting for her daughter, and worshipping with her Lutheran brothers and sisters while she continues to tell her stories.

Maryel is also the author of The Heir of Time Series, a fantasy, YA series set in the ancient Middle East.

**Thank you for choosing Christmas In Other Words! I hope you'll take a moment to leave a rating and a review on Amazon and Goodreads. It would be the best Christmas present!**

Made in the USA
Middletown, DE
06 December 2022

17236701R00057